The
Cat

and Other Stories

Bilingual Press/Editorial Bilingüe

The Cat

and Other Stories
by Beverly Silva

Bilingual Press/Editorial Bilingüe
TEMPE, ARIZONA

ISBN: 0-916950-69-7

Library of Congress Catalog Card Number: 86-70702

PRINTED IN THE UNITED STATES OF AMERICA

Cover design by Christopher J. Bidlack

Acknowledgments

This volume is supported by a grant from the National
Endowment for the Arts in Washington, D.C., a federal
agency.

The story "Poet" first appeared in *Reed* (San José State
University), 1975, pp. 26-28.

Contents

For my children: Geof, Carla, Madelyn, Joy
and for all my professors and friends
at San José State University who aided
me in innumerable ways during the years
when I wrote these stories.

The Cat

I divide the world into cat lovers and cat haters. I have discovered that no matter what people say, deep down in their hearts, no one is indifferent to cats. I had a lot of growing up to do to become a cat lover, and now I test people by their reaction to my cats. Now don't jump to the conclusion that I am one of those eccentric old ladies with eight or ten cats. I once had five cats, but now I only have two, and one of these belongs to my young daughter.

A few months ago I made a resolution that one cat was enough for any woman. With tears in my eyes I set out to find suitable homes for my other three cats. This was not an easy job as cat lovers already had cats, and I could never let a cat hater care for one of my pets out of a sense of pity or obligation. But as determination is one of my weaknesses, within a few days all my cats were comfortably settled.

The reason for my decision to send away those whom I loved came about due to an unexpected and traumatic moment of insight into my personality. I was luxuriously reclining in my pink bath tub full of warm soft bubbles one Saturday evening when my cats started fighting. This annoyed me immensely as I am a softhearted person who wants above all for everyone to love everyone else.

I had a date with Joe that night which I was complacently looking forward to, and I needed time to make myself beautiful for him. While I lay in the tub thinking that if I ignore the noise for awhile perhaps the cats will quiet down, the phone rang. Damn! I keep saying I'll take the phone into the bathroom during moments like this so if it rings I won't have to jump out all drippy and rattled to answer it. Somewhere in the back of my mind, however, is the unanswered fear of whether or not one can be electrocuted by answering a phone while lying in the tub. I keep intending to ask someone about this, but I never remember until I am in the bath tub and the phone rings.

Oh well. I climbed out of my warm retreat all drippy and rattled and answered the phone.

"Yes," I said.

"Hi baby, this is Super Sam."

Pause. Groan. He was drinking again.

Deep male laugh. "You know who this is?"

"Of course. Pete. Your voice is too distinctive to hide."

"Put on something sexy and come over."

Anger. Compassion. "Look Pete, I've told you before you are a charming, brilliant guy, and lots of fun—when you are sober."

"I'm sober, baby."

"Sure, and I'm Marilyn Monroe."

"You sure are."

Pause. Frustration.

"C'mon. Bring me a pot of coffee and I'll promise to behave. We'll listen to Frank Sinatra, and have a quiet evening by the fire."

Temptation. "Pete . . ."

Crash. One of the cats had just knocked over my favorite Italian vase full of straw flowers. Ring. The doorbell. "Pete—hold on."

I walked across the living room careful not to step on the broken pieces of vase, and opened the door a crack. It was Laughing Jack. Standing there in a red turtleneck sweater, tight black slacks, boots, beard, flashing brown eyes, and that everlasting grin. Him you couldn't keep out. He came and went like a falling star.

"Hey," he said in that right on voice of his, "you look fantastic in that towel."

I had forgotten my situation, but then it didn't really matter with Jack.

"Hold on Jack, I'm on the phone."

"Pete . . ."

"What's going on there?" Anger? Pause.

"Hey beautiful, you got a house full of birds or something?"

I stuck my head around the corner towards the kitchenette and saw Jack picking up pieces of bread which the cats had pulled off the table and dragged around the room. Ordinarily I would have laughed. I wondered why I didn't now.

"Are you still there?" It was Pete. More anger? Anxiety?

"Look Pete, a few things have come up."

"You know what, baby. You've got one of the sloppiest minds I've ever seen."

"What!!"

"I said you've got a sloppy mind."

"Well . . . fuck you . . . goodbye." I slammed down the receiver.

Jack was sitting there laughing at me, in my favorite chair, his feet on my glass top coffee table, a glass of my last bottle of imported Spanish wine in his hand. I looked at him closer than usual.

"What do you want?" I asked him. I wanted to be nice, but deep within me the urge to slug someone was asserting itself.

"Get dressed, beautiful. We're going to the jazz concert."

"Did it ever dawn on you I might have other plans?"

"Change them."

Something inside me was beginning to snap. I had wanted to go to that concert all week. I love jazz. I had even considered going alone. On Wednesday, Tom had called to ask what I was doing over the weekend, and I mentioned the concert, but he doesn't dig that kind of thing. Then Friday, Joe had called and invited me to one of those parties he goes to every Saturday night. As my week had not gone well, and I had no other prospects, and my young daughter was spending the weekend with my ex-husband—I refuse to call him her father—what I had once considered a dull evening sounded very pleasant, and I graciously accepted his invitation.

I became aware that I was glaring at Jack while all this churned through my mind. He was looking me up and down as I sat in the wicker rocker I had slumped into after slamming down the phone, with a damp towel wrapped around me and my hair in rollers. He was grinning as usual. Laughing Jack. He reminded me of a character out of Shakespeare, but I couldn't remember which one.

"Look Jack, I really can't go, and I'd like you to leave now."

"O.K., beautiful. You're still the sexiest girl in a towel I ever knew." Out the door he went, laughing as always. I guess he will die laughing.

I shut the door behind him, and locked it. Now why did I do that, I wondered. Oh well, fuck it. The phone rang again. It was Joe. He called to tell me he would be a little late.

Something was coming over me again. "You know what, Joe?"

"What?"

"Just don't bother coming at all."

"Well what the hell gives with you?"

"You. That's what. I find you boring and inconsiderate, and I always have, and I detest those phony parties you go to every week, and I think you're in a rut, and . . ."

He hung up. Men, I growled. Men and their stupid screwed up male egos. Who needs them?

I picked up one of my cats at random and clung to it. It was a fluffy, gray, once-stray, alley cat. It cried and tried to get away. I held it tighter. I sank down on the sofa, and the cat eventually relaxed in my arms and quit fighting. Tears started rolling down my face, slowly at first, then stronger until my whole body was torn with sobbing. I gave in, not asking why, or caring. Hours later I realized I had fallen asleep, and it was dark. My cat was still in my lap, sleeping peacefully.

It was after that I decided one cat was enough for any woman. Hesitantly, may I add, I also decided that one man was enough for any woman, if one could find the right man. And if a woman can find the right cat, I guess she can find the right man.

Poet

He was a terribly nice man. As I spent the evening observing him, I kept imagining that if I decided to crawl in bed with him he would take my hand gently and say, "My dear, it would afford me a great deal of pleasure if you would allow me the privilege of placing my penis in your vagina."

We met at a meeting of the Sexual Freedom League. My girlfriend, who is always trying to find me a respectable and financially well-off boyfriend, explained how cultured he was, and that I simply must attend their Wednesday night orientation meeting. She actually pressed the point so far that it became a matter of give it and/or him a try, or lose a friend.

The meeting was held in his home. He lived alone in a three bedroom house with a grand piano and a twenty-four foot swimming pool. Unfortunately, the leader of the group was ill, and many other members were away on vacation, so very little orientation was possible. Our host read a very long poem he had written about his ideal woman. Everyone liked it very much. His voice was a soft iambic with a slight European accent. The ladies felt the poem contained almost no male chauvinism, and everyone agreed that it expressed love and devotion without the destructive elements of jealousy and possessiveness. I waited patiently for the refreshments, and when the sesame seed cookies and herb tea were served, I began to count the hours of studying I had missed. I looked at my girlfriend and knew there was no way out. Her face was set. She had that "you are going to have a good time and meet nice people even if it kills you" look. I resigned myself to the fact that I could not afford to lose her friendship.

11

I even had to stay when the others left. Our host had been informed that I was doing graduate work in English literature and wanted my honest opinion of his writings. He re-read his poem to me along with others he found in a yellowed folder where he kept his musical compositions. I *was* impressed that he could read for so long in that soft iambic without a few deep breaths, but the nicest thing I could say about his poem was that a few trochees or spondees might add that certain touch. But I smiled at him instead and said, "They are very romantic." He beamed with pleasure.

He told me that his native home was Denmark, which made him much more culturally liberated than Americans, and thus he gave his utmost support to groups like the Sexual Freedom League. He showed me the office where he did freelance engineering and the filing cabinet that contained his patents.

"It's very impressive," I said, which is what I always said when I felt I should be impressed when actually I was bored and understood nothing that was being explained to me. It usually satisfied people.

It did. He took me to the kitchen and removed a very modern uniquely designed fizz bottle from the refrigerator. It contained homemade champagne. He had sold the patent to Paul Masson. The dainty glasses he removed from a shelf held a thimble full of the drink. We sat back on the sofa in his living room where he placed the glasses on a table in front of us which held a large vase of roses, a bunch of blue plastic grapes, and a bronze ashtray with the signs of the zodiac printed along the edge. He continued telling me about his life-style. His hobbies were writing poetry and music, and his socializing consisted of the more advanced singles groups, and occasional work at the Congregational Church.

"You live a very calm and orderly life," was all I could think of saying. My mind was on the untouched glasses in front of us, and I really wanted to say, do we drink this damn champagne or inhale it.

"You see," he continued, "God endowed me with this creativity, and I feel it is my duty to protect it. I do not smoke, I rarely drink, and I avoid extremes of any kind."

It's not always easy for me to keep my mouth shut and remember propriety. "Some of our greatest American writers were horrible drunks," I commented.

"Oh, Americans," he replied with the "Oh" coming close to a trochee sound.

I was forming a long list of European geniuses who were drunks, dopers, whorers, and everything else I could think of, when he asked me a question.

"Are you creative?"

I took the glass of champagne without an invitation and drank it as slowly as one can drink a thimble full of liquid while I dug deep for an answer. "Well, I do write some," I told him, "but my writings would probably be considered more as sociological documents than creative literature. They lack the romanticism of your poetry."

He moved closer to me. "It is so agreeable to meet an educated and appreciative woman," he stated.

Fuck propriety. "Do you think I could have a little more champagne?" I asked him.

"Of course," he said rising and taking my glass to the kitchen. "How thoughtless of me."

He returned with another thimble full of the liquid. He placed it on the table. I picked it up, feeling like a very ill-bred woman, but also feeling somewhat more secure.

He once again moved closer to me. "In spite of my group involvements," he confided to me, "I'm really quite shy with women."

I finished drinking the champagne, and then carefully studied the glass.

He moved all the way towards me now, removed the glass from my hand, set it on the table, put his arm around my shoulder, and took my hand in his.

Before I could obey my impulse to retrieve my hand and rise, he looked me directly in the eyes for the first time, and had they always been that cold and blue? And he said to me, "Do you suck?"

I jumped up quickly, saying, "Excuse me for a moment," and went to the kitchen. I reached into the first cupboard I saw, and luck was with me. I removed a very ordinary water glass. I opened the refrigerator and removed the fizz bottle. Pushing the button all the way down I soon had a large glass of champagne. Evidently my host was still on the sofa waiting for an answer. I leaned against the kitchen counter and drank the entire glass. I then returned to the living room.

He was on the sofa, much like a contented rabbit, showing no curiosity about my sudden departure. I looked him firmly in the eyes.

"Are you aware that your last words changed from iambic to a definite anapest?" I asked him.

He sat up startled, his eyes blinking at me, and his nose definitely twitching.

There appeared to be no way out of this now except through the English teacher route, sophomorish as it was. "American writers," I told him, "often use very extreme language. In my own writings, for example, I make use of a strong spondee. Fuck you!"

I then excused myself by claiming a mild case of gastritis brought on by the champagne, and I left. I drove to the nearest bar where I met a man who assured me he had never tasted sesame seed cookies. He bought me five brandy alexanders while I told him the whole sordid tale of my favorite uncle who was found knifed by his third wife's lover. We went to his apartment later. He wasn't very cultured, but he was a terribly nice man.

The Thesis

Gary awoke slowly and edged his arm over the sheet seeking for Pat's body. Drowsily he realized she was gone. At work. She had a job now to supplement their income. He dozed off again with a feeling of emptiness. When sleep would no longer come, he turned over onto his back and lay there staring around the room. A sudden laugh rose in him as he mumbled, "That crazy woman." Who else, he reflected, would decorate a bedroom with pink ruffled curtains, an orange striped Indian rug, purple furniture, a scarlet incense burner, a black candle in a gold holder, a poster of Emiliano Zapata alongside one of Jonathon Livingston Seagull, and a La Raza calendar over their bed. Well, that's what you get when you marry a screwed-up history major. One day she's yelling about revolution and boycotts, and the next she's nagging about unpaid bills and wanting a new dress. And she can't do a thing right. He looked at the purple dresser with the uneven blotchy paint. His mind went back to the week they had moved in this apartment.

"It's a mess. A goddam mess," Pat had said with slight outrage at her first sight of their new home. It was University City #32 and they had waited almost a year to get in.

"What do you expect for $97.50 a month?" Gary had said defensively.

"I expect YOU to paint this damn place before I move one thing in," she answered while poking him in the chest with her index finger.

"Me?" he said indignantly, "I've got to work on my thesis."

"And I've got three mid-terms in the next two weeks," she said.

Somehow they had compromised. He spent one weekend

and a couple of evenings painting while she scrubbed floors and fixtures. He had been forced to admit the previous tenants must have been doing research with the place full of baboons.

Two days after they moved in he came home from an early morning trip to the library and found her with all the bedroom furniture, which consisted of odd pieces they had collected over a near year of marriage, in one corner of the room with a few newspapers and a can of lavender spray paint. She was on her knees in a pair of jeans and one of his T-shirts spraying away and humming an old blues tune.

Gary stepped into the room and jumped back startled. "Good God woman, what are you doing?"

"You dig?" she asked sweetly.

"Like a fumigated whore house," he answered while crossing the room to the one window. "Did it ever dawn on you this stuff can be lethal?"

He pushed at the window which sprang back at him. "How do you prop the window open, Pat?" he asked, a little subdued now.

"I think the neighbors use iron rods," she answered with a tinge of sarcasm. "I've tried everything else. Which reminds me, I was hoping you'd get home to do some shopping. We need a few things—like iron rods for a start. We have four windows in this apartment, all of which won't stay open with coat hangers, or sticks, or anything else I've tried." She stood up looking him directly in the eyes.

He stared back at her defiantly until both of them burst out laughing and flopped onto the mattress which had been shoved to one side of the room while she painted.

"You damn nut," he said, staring again into those sassy brown eyes he could never resist. "If we're going to live in a purple whore house, let's enjoy it."

That was almost a year ago and since then she had made this converted army barrack called student housing into a livable home. Gary whimsically remembered the gallons of paint, rolls of contact paper, Pat's nutty posters, and paper lamp shades they had shopped for. Yep, she was a nut and never did anything right. The paint was a mess, the contact paper was placed on the shelves and bookcases crooked, and the living room lamp shade hung lopsided by a piece of string. Patience and perfectionism were definitely lacking in her character. She even made so many errors in typing his papers that he had finally stopped asking her.

Abruptly Gary put all this out of his mind and crossing his arms over his head, he began to plan his day before getting up. Where to start? The same old problem. Let's see, his train of thought went, shall I head for the kitchen and see if Pat made coffee and left me a note? Or shall I cross the four feet to the pack of Winstons lying on the dresser and have a smoke? Or I could just stay in bed awhile and indulge in some horny fantasies.

He finally decided on the Winstons, took a couple of drags, and pulled a pair of levis up over his long muscular legs. Then, after stretching and scratching his tan and lightly-haired chest, he headed for the kitchen.

He looked at the old gas stove and plastic kitchen table. "That bitch," he said aloud. No coffee, and no note. Instead, last night's dishes were all over the place along with a jar of instant coffee and box of corn flakes Pat had used before leaving. Just because she has a job now, he thought, she thinks she's so important. Better do something here before she gets too sassy. Never let a woman get the upper hand. She only has three night classes and a four day a week job at the bookstore. Leaves her plenty of time to keep things up around here. She knows how pressed I am finishing my thesis.

Fumbling in his levis for a match, Gary then lit the gas stove and filled a saucepan with water for his coffee. Next, he crossed the ten-foot living room and stared out the window. It was lightly raining and no one was in sight. Only the long clothes line with a few faded towels someone had left out from yesterday met his eyes. He passed his gaze beyond these to the other rows of army barracks. Nothing going on today, he mused.

Walking back to the kitchen, he made a cup of instant coffee with two teaspoonfuls of sugar and told himself to get to work. In the living room on a long coffee table painted bright green, one of Pat's flea market prizes she had also sprayed, sat his typewriter and papers. He sank onto the gold corduroy sofa in front of his work and picked up page eighty-two of his thesis: *The Correlation of I.Q. to Sexual Satisfaction in the Human Female.* He read the last paragraph.

> Anne's and Betty's score on employment satisfaction as assessed by *S* questionnaire and level of arousal as assessed by GSR taken together are approximately one standard deviation below the mean of the total group of *Ss*.

Not satisfied with that, Gary thought. Think I'll spend today doing pure research to straighten out a few kinks. He glanced at the pile of books on the floor. Pushing aside the hardbacks he rummaged among the paperbacks until he came to a thin one by Greenwald entitled *The Call Girl.* He glanced over the table of contents and read, "Psychological factors influencing the choice of the profession—page 107." Turning to the page, he picked up his cup and found the coffee was gone. Shit, he growled, a man can't work on an empty stomach. If I eat better, it will nourish my brain.

He walked back to the kitchen and looked dismally at the corn flakes. Rejecting those, he opened the old refrigerator, being careful not to scratch his hand on the broken chrome handle. Got to file this down one of these days, he thought. He surveyed the contents inside. Half a bottle of Red Mountain wine, an almost empty carton of milk, an unopened package of tortillas, three jars of jalapenos, a quart of mayonnaise, catsup, cocktail onions, four plastic dishes of leftovers, one dish of diet margarine, half a pitcher of orange juice, and one egg. Withdrawing the orange juice, Gary reached above the sink to the old wood cabinet painted green like the coffee table and got out a glass and a bottle of one-a-day vitamins. Filling the glass and tossing two vitamins into his mouth, he gulped them down with the juice and proceeded to look out the back window. A large chain fence was twelve feet away and beyond that was an open field used as a parking lot on game nights. At the corner beyond that, the traffic light blinked from red to green and a few cars passed by. He felt a slight surge of envy for the occupants, wherever they were going.

His mind went back to the refrigerator. One fucking egg! Think I'll go downtown. Haven't treated myself to breakfast for a long time. Besides the exercise will do me good. Stimulate my brain.

Thus convinced, Gary went to the bedroom and threw on an old blue turtleneck sweater over his levis, slipped on a pair of basketball shoes, and ran a comb over his shaggy, desert-colored, longish hair and his longer and shaggier beard. Waiting outside the back door, chained to the porch rail, was his bike. It was an old one, but a good one, he thought, remembering how he was fortunate to get it off the black market for $40 last summer when bikes were impossible to find, and his had been ripped off. No one will touch this one with so many new ones around and especially with this chain. As he pedaled down the street, he realized how he missed that shiny new red one he had before, and still felt angry that the police didn't do more about all the stealing and dealing that went on in this neighborhood.

Arriving at his favorite restaurant after the mile and a half ride, he felt stimulated and hungry and realized as he pushed open the door that he was cheerful now where he hadn't been before. He surveyed the booths to see if anyone he knew was there. There wasn't, so he chose a seat at the counter. An attractive blonde waitress around thirty years old placed coffee in front of him.

"Hi Gary," she said warmly, "haven't seen you for a week or so."

Gary smiled at her. "Miss me, huh? You're looking fabulous, Alice. How's the new husband?"

"Two months old and doing well," she answered.

"Still honeymooning?"

She laughed and gave him a firm look. "You mind your own business. I know you psychology students. Always prying into people's private affairs. Sometimes I think all of you are sex maniacs."

"We are," Gary said calmly.

"Oh, shut up," she answered, shoving a menu at him and walking away.

He watched her moving, enjoying the way her ass twisted and the muscles in her legs tightened when she bent over. Wish I'd screwed her when I had a chance, he thought. Wonder what she's like? Then his mind went back to Pat. Hell, she's gone three nights a week and all day. What good is she? If I had a little more sex it would relieve tension and I'd work better.

When Alice placed bacon and eggs in front of him she asked about his paper.

"It's going great," Gary answered. "I was up all night working on it. Should have it ready for publication in a month."

She looked at him with admiration. "I don't know how you do it. I always wanted to go to college, but just didn't have the brains."

Gary looked intently into her slightly puzzled-looking green eyes. "That reminds me, Alice," he said coolly, "I always wanted to do an I.Q. on you. Could you help me out with some research when you're off?"

She flashed her eyes on him all bristly waitress again. "You get lost. I've heard of you and your research!"

Gary laughed and began on his eggs. He left a twenty-five cent tip for Alice and headed for home on his bike. On the way, he began thinking about Mary. They had once lived together for a brief period. Maybe I'll go see her today. Pat's gone all the time, and she'll never know. With this in mind, he rode a little faster.

After arriving home, Gary went to the bedroom and began rummaging through drawers trying to remember where his old phone book was. When he and Pat got married, they had made a pact to save their old phone numbers to help avoid that trapped feeling married people get. After searching the entire desk and four dresser drawers, he found the book beneath his clean underwear. It was a small black book with the edges unglued and curling. He held it with a feeling of excitement, and telling himself to play it cool now, he automatically went toward the kitchen where he removed the Red Mountain from the refrigerator and poured a generous glassful.

Sitting back on the sofa, he moved the phone next to him and thumbed through the book. There it was. Mary Rojas—258-1600. He sipped on the wine, set the glass down slowly next to his typewriter, and dialed the number.

"Hello," a feminine voice answered.

"Hello there; is Mary in today?"

"Who?"

"Mary. Mary Rojas."

"Never heard of her." The voice sounded impatient.

Gary frowned and gathered his warmest tone. "Is this 258-1600?"

"Yes."

"And Mary Rojas doesn't live there?"

"Nope."

"And you don't know her?"

"Nope."

Hmmm. "How long have you lived there?"

"Six months, and what business is it of yours?"

Gary paused and took a long breath. "You know, you have a very unusual voice."

"Huh?"

"I hope you will forgive me for being so open," he continued, "but your voice is so unique, so sensuous, and exciting, I can't help but wonder what type of woman you are."

"Yeah?" There was a mixture of doubt and curiosity in her voice.

Gary leaned back with a sigh. He was grooving now. "Tell me about yourself," he said softly.

Her tone of impatience was definitely gone. "Oh, I'm nothing special."

"Are you a student?"

"Yes. My first year here."

"You must be a drama major with that voice."

She giggled now. "No, I'm in nursing."

"Nursing! That connects. A real woman's profession."

"You really think so?"

"Definitely!"

"What do you do?" she asked.

"I'm a grad student," he answered in a matter-of-fact way.

"Yeah. And what's your major?"

"Psychology. I'm getting my thesis ready for publication this month."

"Really! How impressive," she said.

"But that's not important," Gary answered. "What matters is that two souls, on a lonely day, by chance, happened to find each other."

"Huh?" she said, and after a long pause, "hey, you some kind of a kook?"

"I'm a sex maniac," Gary answered.

She hung up.

Gary doubled over with laughter. He hadn't enjoyed himself so much for days. He sipped on the wine and read through the old phone book remembering past pleasures and mentally marking a few numbers to check later.

Throwing the book aside impulsively, Gary mumbled, "Think I'll see what Tony is doing." Tony was his next door neighbor. Another social science nut, but he plays a good guitar, was how Gary defined him.

He went out the door and crossed the short porch to his neighbor's, stopping at the door. A sign, DO NOT DISTURB, was hanging there. Well, Gary reflected, he's either screwing or studying.

Returning to his apartment feeling downcast, Gary moved again automatically to the kitchen and refilled his glass with wine, noticing that the bottle was nearly empty. Hope Pat stops at the store: we need some groceries in this place.

He began pacing the living room trying to block from his mind the awesome typewriter sitting there like a mechanical monster waiting to suck away his life's blood. Looking again out the window he noticed the mailman pass. There was a slight lift in his spirits. Never know what the mail may bring. He went out and reached into the rusty box withdrawing two envelopes, and three loose papers. He returned to the sofa with mail and wine and got into a comfortable position with his long legs stretched out across the table next to his typewriter.

First, the envelopes. Pacific Gas and Electric. No need to open that, and he tossed it aside. The other was from school. He opened it with curiosity, and began reading: "Dear student, Our records show that you will be leaving the University this semester. It is necessary that I have a personal interview with you in order to set up a repayment schedule for your Federally Insured Student Loans, and explain certain rights and obligations that are of concern to you."

Gary yawned and tossed this letter aside also. He then picked up the papers. The first was a political candidate asking for his vote. No news here, and it was laid aside. The next was an announcement of a new pizza parlor and a coupon giving 30% off on a giant pizza. He carefully slid it under his typewriter. The last paper was a hand printed list of household belongings for sale in Apt. #21 whose occupants were returning to Arabia. Gary sighed, "back to the great work."

He picked up Greenwald's book and began to read page 107: "After the twenty girls had been interviewed, I found I had amassed a large amount of material"—then he rose, book still in hand, and, continuing to read, went into the bedroom for a pillow. Placing it at the end of the sofa, he reclined into his favorite position. His left leg was thrown up over the sofa back and against the wall, while his right leg was straight on the sofa and his foot pushed at the strip of wood on the edge. With the book propped on his chest, he continued reading while his fingers groped across the coffee table searching for his package of cigarettes. He found it and dug inside discovering emptiness. Placing the book face down on the table, he began a search for another package. When the kitchen cupboards, the desk and dresser drawers, the space under the bed, the sofa, and his typewriter did not yield even one long butt, he decided a trip to the store was a necessity.

Gary rode his bike the four blocks to the liquor store and pushed open the glass doors. No one was inside. He went to the counter and banged on a bell while shouting, "Hey, Sam, you got a customer."

A middle-aged man with a large build and a W. C. Fields face came out of the back room.

"Having a snort, Sam?" Gary asked with a grin.

"Inventory, Gary, you know how it is with a business," the man answered.

"Sure, Sam."

"How's your paper coming?" Sam directed the conversation to Gary.

"Great," he answered, "been working on it since early this morning. Plan to have it all ready for publication in a few weeks."

"I don't know how you students do it," Sam replied, "spending all your time in those books."

"Well, different strokes for different folks," Gary said.

Sam shook his head in a bewildered manner. "What will it be today?"

"Two packs of Winstons."

"Anything else?"

Gary thought it over. He had a long day of research ahead of him. One of the guys might drop over. "Yeah. Give me a 6-Pack of Bud."

Back home, Gary opened a beer, threw a few tortillas on the gas burner, and rummaged in the combination pantry-storage room which was supposed to compensate for the lack of closets and storage in this temporary home, until he found a can of sardines. With a plate full of sardine tacos and a beer in hand, Gary stepped over the vacuum cleaner and made his way back to the living room sofa where he returned to page 107 of the book he was researching.

One hour and two beers later, his head began to nod, and he became drowsily aware of music from a nearby apartment. Time for a stretch to keep awake, and he pulled his near-six feet up and out onto the porch.

He stood on the porch stretching and trying to locate the music. No one was in sight, and Tony's sign was still on the door. "This place is really dead today," he mumbled, sitting on the damp step. He glanced down the row of buildings. Wonder what hours that new chick in #28 keeps. I'd like to meet her. Think her old man works nights. I need to spend more time socializing. Check hours people come and go.

Gary re-entered his apartment and turned on the stereo, twisting the dials until he found a tune that satisfied him. Lou Rawls was singing "A Natural Man." "Oldie but Goodie," Gary mused as he began tapping his feet and gyrating his hips to the music. "Right on," he said loudly, when Lou sang out, "I'm going to taste it now before I die." Four tunes later, Gary switched off the stereo and sank back on the sofa with a fresh can of beer. Wonder what Al's doing, and he reached for the phone and dialed. There was no answer. The old phone book he had thrown aside caught his attention and he picked it up. Sipping on his beer, he again thumbed through it. Margie Smith stood out in large print. He tried to remember her, and couldn't. He let his mind flow over a long list of vague remembrances. It stopped finally with the picture of a sun tanned girl who played volleyball. That's her, and he dialed the number without further thought.

"Hello." It was a man's voice.

"Hello there. I'm inquiring after an old friend. Margery Smith. Is she in by chance?"

"No, she isn't. Who's calling?"

"Oh, it's not important. I'm just an old friend passing through town."

"Do you want to leave a message?"

Gary definitely did not like that voice. "If you will, please," he said, "Just tell her that Thomas Valentino, an old admirer, was in town, and immediately remembered a very charming woman he used to know."

"O.K." The man hung up.

Gary grinned and leaned back with his beer. Margie Smith. He remembered her now. Majoring in P.E. and great in bed. Wonder what that dude on the phone is like?

Reclining back in his favorite position again, Gary picked up *The Call Girl* and began reading. Within twenty minutes his head was nodding on his chest and the book had slipped to the floor.

He awoke with a start and a cramp in his neck. Sitting up abruptly and rubbing his neck, he thought, "I really should do all this research at the library. Home is no place to work." Then he remembered the last time he had planned to work at the library and had made it only to the entrance. Little Joe had sat there on a bench like a guardian bulldog keeping away all but the holiest. They had rapped and then ended up at Al's pad boozing it up. Gary frowned, and wondered if he was one of those people who couldn't say no. He ruminated over various psychological theories, and then remembered the number one rule. A psychologist must never apply psychology to himself. That settled it.

For the first time that day, he wondered what time it was. "Good God," he said aloud, after walking to the kitchen to see the wall clock. "It's 4:45 already." Pat would be home in less than a half hour. He gave the kitchen a sad look. I really should wash up these dishes, but shit, that's a woman's job. Think I'll rewrite that last page of my manuscript and call it a day. He shoved the beer cans into the paper bag of garbage under the sink, pressing down to make room for future needs, then reached for the refrigerator. "Damn," he said, jerking his now bleeding hand away from the jagged chrome handle. "I am going to fix that today." Sucking the blood from the injured hand, he used his good one to cautiously open the door and remove the wine bottle. There wasn't enough left for a glass. He tipped his head back and finished the contents, then tossed the bottle on top of the beer cans. His hand had stopped bleeding by now. He opened a beer and went back to the sofa.

Al was certain to have a file. Gary picked up the phone and dialed.

"Al, hey man, haven't seen you in days. What's the latest? What? You're screwing? You're putting me on. Wait. Don't hang up. Have you got a . . ."

Some friend he is. Gary dialed Little Joe's number. "Joe, where ya' been? Yeah. Yeah. Yeah. Uh-huh. Say, I need a file. File—that's it. No, I haven't forgotten about the V.W. parts. Have them Saturday. Definitely. Could you drop it by tonight? That late? O.K. See you then. Wait! If no one answers put it in the mailbox. The MAILBOX. Yeah. Thanks man."

He hung up satisfied and reached under the coffee table for a clean piece of typing paper. Inserting it in the machine, he gave deep consideration to the best wording to summarize page eighty-two.

The back door banged open and Pat descended upon him. "Is the genius hard at work?" she asked.

Gary slowly raised his head to look at her. She appeared six feet tall standing there with her legs spread apart and her hands on her hips. He surveyed her from the brown leather sandals, long shapely legs, and neat pink dress, up to her crazy dangling earrings and long brown hair twisted back in a bun. My God, she did things to his guts, and was she smiling or laughing at him with those soft pink lips and sassy eyes?

"You home already?" he said casually.

She leaned over the typewriter. "Let's see what's new."

Gary had a strong urge to protectively cover his work. "I just started a new page," he told her. "I've been doing research all day."

"Oh," was all she said. Then, "Maybe you can do some research around this dump while I shower and change." She retreated into the bathroom, and Gary sat still staring at nothing until he heard the water running.

He rose with a tinge of guilt and went into the kitchen. Gathering up cans and papers and leftover scraps of food, he threw them all into the paper bag and headed out the back door towards the garbage cans at the far end of the building. On the way he met Tony. He found out he had been studying that day and not screwing. He had an exam at seven that evening. Gary began feeling depressed and that made him angry.

When he was back in the apartment, he sat upright and began busily retyping page eighty-two. The keys clicked noisily as he waited for Pat to come out of the bedroom where she was dressing.

She finally appeared and sat opposite him in their one chair. It was square and went with the sofa so to speak, but she had covered it in orange corduroy insisting they needed contrasting colors. She was barefoot now, and had changed into jeans and a loose flowered shirt. Why do women wear a dress to work and come home and put on jeans, Gary wanted to ask someone. He was satisfied to see her hair hanging loose and flowing the way he liked it, however. She sat there puffing on a cigarette, looking at him, and saying nothing.

"What's for dinner?" he asked her.

"That's a good question," she answered.

Damn. That woman is too much! Gary looked down at his typewriter feigning indifference. "I'm going to finish a few more pages before I call it a day," he told her. He began busily typing.

Pat put out her cigarette and reached for another, playing with it but not lighting it. She was tired from shelving books all day: she had spent last night in class, had another class tomorrow night, and should spend tonight reading at least a hundred pages on the diplomatic relations between the U.S. and Mexico before World War I. She lit the cigarette in her hand and sat there brooding. When it was smoked down to the filter, she crushed it out and stepped into the kitchen. She glared at the array of dirty dishes piled on the table, stove, one small counter top, and in the sink. She moved to the refrigerator, opened the door, and looked in. With a sad silent look she slowly closed the door and turned back towards the sink. She reached down and picked up a dirty creamy-white plate with a sick-green stripe around the edge. It was part of the second-hand dishes Gary's aunt had given them. She raised it up slowly and then forcefully banged it over the old-fashioned water faucet watching the pieces fly. She reached for another plate with a gleeful look in her eyes. Crash!

Gary was on his feet and across the room. "What the hell are you doing?"

"Breaking a few dishes, that's all." She smiled sweetly at him.

"You flipping your lid?"

"Yep." Crash went another plate.

"And what about my dinner?"

"YOUR dinner?" Another crash.

"Woman, you are up-tight." Gary was torn between anger and laughter as he removed another dish from her hand.

She didn't resist, but shouted at him now, "Don't you think I get tired of washing these fucking dishes? Why can't you do them?"

"Do I ask you to do my work?" Gary answered her in a matter-of-fact way.

"Your work," she said in a quieter tone. "Do you mean that goddam thesis? For over a year, all I hear is your great masterpiece, but all I see is you reaching for a bottle."

Gary resisted the urge to slug her. "You bitch," he shouted.

"You bastard," she shouted back.

He grabbed her arm and forced her to the living room pushing her back into the chair. "Now you sit there and cool off," he said with finality. "I'll fix you a drink."

Gary groped through the pantry shelves certain there was a bottle somewhere. Finally, behind a can of refried beans, auto wax, and toilet bowl cleaner, he found a fifth of Seagram's. It was two-thirds full. He went to the kitchen filling two glasses with ice, water, and a liberal amount of whiskey.

"Here," he said to Pat, shoving the glass at her.

She took it without saying a word. He sat back on the sofa, and they gave each other long silent looks.

Gary gave in first. "Oh hell, Pat, I've been bored silly. Let's fuck."

"You really know how to turn a woman on," she answered with that intent look in her eyes that nearly drove him mad.

He stared back at her. "Well, if you don't want to fuck, I'm going to listen to music and get drunk."

"Think I'll join you this time." She took a long drink.

"Go right ahead."

Gary rose and went to the stereo turning the dial to his favorite station. The Oldies but Goodies were still playing. Carole King sang out, "It's Too Late."

He sat back on the sofa and looked at Pat. She had her legs draped over the edge of the chair, her drink was almost gone, and she was swinging her legs to the music now. She was not looking at him.

He broke the silence again. "You do look sexy sitting like that—from across the room, that is."

She turned her gaze on him coolly. "I know it."

"Still a bitch," he shot out.

"And a bastard," she answered. She then rose and fixed herself another drink placing the bottle on the floor next to her chair.

They sat in silence again listening to the music. Gary began ruminating over the good old days before all this woman's lib came about. No woman would dare sit there like that then. "Pass the fucking bottle," he blurted out.

Pat turned her head towards him slowly, picked up the bottle and said, "Catch," while it was soaring across the room towards him.

He fumbled but caught it and held it tight against his chest. "Hey," he yelled at her, "that's all we've got."

"You always know how to get more."

"That's right."

More silence. She broke it this time. "Give me another drink."

"You've had enough."

"Who says?"

"I do. You know you can't hold it."

"I know who will give me more," she said with a wild look of defiance.

"You always were a bitch!"

"You said yourself he wanted to make out with me and why didn't I."

"Who?" Gary asked with an indifferent tone, although he knew who.

"Joe." She was really challenging him now.

Gary challenged her back. "Call him."

She crossed the room and picked up the phone from the sofa next to Gary and brought it to her chair, sitting back with it in her lap. She dialed slowly.

Gary had a mental picture of Joe picking up the phone and answering, "Little Joe speaking," in that husky voice.

"Hi Joe," he heard Pat say, "guess who . . ."

Crash! Gary had lunged across the room and knocked the phone out of her hand. It hit the edge of the bookcase and lay on the floor with the receiver cracked and split open.

"You maniac," Pat shouted, "that will cost twenty dollars!"

"Shut up and have another drink." He leaned over her, fill-ing the glass in her hand half full of whisky.

She was going on and on about the phone. "You know we can't afford it. You *are* insane. When we met, I thought you were cute. Always on the phone. In every room. Carrying it around while you talked. Research you called it. I soon found out what that meant. Twenty-five foot cord. The damn phone goes ten feet outside both of our doors. And it *will* cost twenty dollars, at least."

"Oh shut up and drink." Gary turned the volume up on the stereo and sank back on the sofa. Frank Sinatra was singing now. "I did it my way," rang out as he and Pat sat in silence once again stealing occasional angry looks at each other.

Gary felt like an eternity was passing by. Pat might be loaded by now, but her eyes had that never-wavering look still. He could stand it no longer. Impulsively, he rose and sat on the floor in the middle of the room. Pat was watching him closely. All his desire burst forth as he said, "I'll meet you halfway."

Pat was on the floor with his chest pinning her down and her arms clinging to him as he was tugging at her jeans. "Where's that goddam zipper?"

She reached down. "You just broke it."

He finished pulling until her jeans were past her hips, and she wiggled out of them while he slipped his levis off.

"Take off that damn sweater," she insisted while pulling her blouse over her head.

Both of them were nude now and Gary kissed her long and hard feeling a calmness and control return to him. "We could get in bed," he whispered.

"Let's not," she answered.

He lowered himself on top of her gently, his penis finding her as naturally as metal drawn to a magnet. Oh God, he was thinking, I'm so hooked on this woman no other could begin to satisfy me. If she finds that out, I'm done for.

Pat was breathing hard beneath him. She was twenty-four and had had her share of lovers before him, but no one had made her feel like this. He was large and he went deep, and she didn't care what anyone's theories about sexual methods and needs were, he was just all himself and all with it, even through their fights. It made a difference. It really did.

He was gently but forcefully grinding and thrusting away at

her. She was moaning and digging her fingers into his back. He was being careful and waiting for the right moment. He felt her trembling. "Are you ready?" he said softly.

She took a long breath. "Yes. Yes," she told him.

Gary poured all his strength into that last effort and felt himself slipping away into the darkness where he always called her name.

She was limp beneath him now with tears running down her face.

"Honey. Why are you crying?" Warmth and concern poured from him.

Her arms slipped around his neck. "You crazy, crazy man. Where could I ever replace you?" She kissed his forehead and nose and both cheeks, then said, "Now please move your big, bearded body off me."

He rolled off slowly and lay quietly next to her.

"I want a blanket, Gary," she said nudging him.

He got up and walked to the bedroom while she watched his naked body knowing full well her power over him.

He tucked the blanket around her thinking what a baby she was and lay beside her cradling her head on his chest.

"Pat," he whispered, "I'm going to finish my thesis next month. Really I am."

"I know, Gary, I know," she answered with tears beginning to form again, "I've never doubted you."

A Small Western Town

A small town in the West was mentioned on the morning news, and my ears pricked up, for I had lived in this town an eon ago when I stood on the threshold of life as an eighteen-year-old just out of school. I have no fond memories of this town for it was a depressed, distressed, small western town of seasonal employment, where the men worked in the woods all summer and lived on State Compensation all winter. The fortunate, or ambitious, ones, held the few year-round jobs driving trucks, but they too lived in the drab houses that made this clearing in the woods a town, and spent their leisure time and money in the local taverns. The main highway that led from the city to the State College, and then on to the coast, went through the middle of this town, and the drivers would have to slow down for the few block expanse of the business district, but there was no reason for anyone to stop. In fact, there was really little reason to obey the thirty-five mile-per-hour sign posted at the edge of town, because on Sunday, the day of the most traffic, the businesses were closed. The town consisted of a dozen various shops, two restaurants, three drug stores, and one movie theater, all closed on Sunday for this was a religious town where the people boasted that they had more churches per person than any other town in the State. For every church, however, there lay a tavern on one of the roads outside the town limits, for the town itself was dry. In the evenings you could find children asleep in the cars lining the tavern parking lots while their parents were inside gossiping, playing shuffleboard, and drinking tap beer. Whiskey was not sold over the bar in those days. On Saturday night you could count on a brawl before the night was over, which usually began over one of the men finding his wife or girlfriend out with someone else.

Yes, I have no happy memories of this town, but when you are eighteen, happiness exists even in your unhappiness, and life holds a promise somewhere in the unknown future. When I moved to Newburg, I knew no one except my elderly great aunt whom I moved in with. I had turned eighteen years of age, had graduated from high school the past month, and now I was free. I felt less like a relative living with my aunt, and more like a boarder in a lonely, aged, but well-kept house. I paid my aunt seven dollars a week for room and board, and I spent my time in her home almost always alone in my room, afraid to muss the heavily starched curtains or leave a mark from a coke bottle on the massive mahogany furniture, and only smoking after ten o'clock in the evening when my aunt had retired for the night. At this time I would stretch out on the high four-poster bed, sink into the downy mattress, slowly inhale a cigarette, and survey the room. My eyes always traveled to the high ceiling, the heavy dark molding around this ceiling, and the four pictures that were hung with faded golden cord from this molding. One was a picture of Jesus at the Last Supper. One was a sleeping baby with an angel hovering over its crib, all done in blue and gold, except for the pink face of the sleeping infant. Another was a shepherd with his flock, done in subdued autumn hues, and my favorite was a large picture with four black and white portraits of my great uncles as young men. They wore the clothes of around 1900; one of the men had especially rakish eyes, and I delighted in making up stories about him. When I tired of this, I would reflect on my own life. I was lonely, but free. I had wanted this for a long time, and it was enough for now. I had a job in the city working at a department store, and the twenty-mile bus ride gave me time to read the many books I desired. I arrived home in the evening content to just breathe the summer air that flowed through the stiff old-fashioned curtains, lie on that huge bed, daydream, and reflect on my newfound freedom and the fact of my existence.

Half the summer passed in this way. Then the restlessness overcame me. I began spending all that was left of my meager salary after expenses on books, for I loathed reading library books, and I had a strong need to possess something of my own. One can read of other people's lives for only so long, however, without a desire to experience life for oneself. I then started staying in the city after work, eating my dinner out, and walking the crowded streets, feeling a part of the bustling, sophisticated life that surrounded me. This was not satisfactory, however, because the last bus for Newburg left at eight p.m., and I had to be on it. There was still a lonely evening facing me when I arrived home. Next, I began going to the local movie twice a week, but this only increased my desire to be living. The day I was informed my services were no longer needed at the department store, it was with a sense of exhilaration that I clocked out for the last time. The future was again mine to seek.

My first sense of exhilaration soon changed to aimlessness, and, not knowing what else to do, I again sought work in the city. Two days went by filling out applications, and being told I would be notified when they had an opening. As my enthusiasm for working as a salesclerk wasn't great, this didn't dishearten me. On the third day, I bumped into a school friend.

"Julie," she shouted, "it's so great to see you. What *have* you been doing all summer?"

Before I could answer, she began telling me about her summer. "We spent three fabulous weeks down at the coast. George, and Betty, and Marilyn, and Bob, and well, you know, the whole gang were there. We had a fabulous time! And remember Ron Jeppson, who graduated a year ago?"

This wasn't phrased in the form of a question, but more as a pronouncement, and she didn't notice my weak smile and nod, but leaned close in a confidential way and continued, "Well— don't say anything yet, but we are sort of engaged."

With this statement she beamed like one who had just received a blue ribbon at the county fair. Before I had time to congratulate her, her mother bore down on us. A rather heavy, middle-aged woman dressed all in beige, including her gloves and hat, she made a sharp contrast with her daughter's gay pink dress and dark suntanned skin. Her voice was impatient as she said, "Patricia, we *must* be going. We have so much shopping to do. You know this is our last day before school starts."

Then noticing me, she said, "Oh, hello—uh—"

"Julie, mother." Patricia broke in. "You remember her. The smartest girl in school."

I tried to protest, but Patricia laughed and continued, "Well anyway, I never could have passed old Morrison's lit. class without her."

"How are you, Julie?" The older woman inquired in a somewhat distracted manner.

"Fine, thank you, Mrs. Rogers," I said automatically, feeling very uncomfortable.

"Are you ready for school?" she continued while glancing at her watch.

"I graduated this year, and now I'm . . ." looking for a job, I tried to say, but Patricia stopped me.

"Gee Julie, it was great to see you," she said. "We simply have to get together again."

After they had left, the day was ruined for me. I no longer had the heart to seek employment. The shop windows full of back-to-school clothes glared at me, and I wondered why I hadn't particularly noticed them before.

I returned home and flopped on the four-poster, no longer interested in the pictures on the wall, and no longer caring if cigarette smoke seeped under the door while my aunt had not yet retired.

For the rest of the day and all the following one, I stayed in my room and re-read *The Return of the Native*, identifying fully with Eustacia Vye. When the late-summer darkness descended, I slowly walked the two miles from one end of town to the other, avoiding the few lighted streets, and imagined myself on the lonely heath.

I awoke early the next morning and took stock of my possessions. Besides my few clothes and toilet articles, all I owned were a shabby photograph album full of pictures of high school friends, old valentines, a few souvenirs from my trip to Los Angeles when I was sixteen, a pressed gardenia from the Senior prom, my graduation announcement, and eighteen books, four of which were hard cover. These were *The Rubaiyat of Omar Khayyam*, and the complete works of Byron, Shelley, and Keats. I had bought these, one each week, with the first money I'd earned that summer. Examining further, I probed into my handbag and discovered I had a half package of cigarettes, and $23.87. These were my total possessions.

Without bothering with breakfast, I walked downtown and bought a bus ticket to Centerville, where the State College was

located. Sinking back in the stiff, cracked upholstery of the Greyhound bus, I asked myself what I was doing. I could find no
answer except, just looking. All I wanted was to see what it
looked like, because I'd never seen a college.

It wasn't hard to find when I arrived, for it sat in the middle
of town with an ivy-covered tower and green sloping lawns dot-
ted with huge maple trees. It was still early in the morning, and
no one was around. I approached with a feeling of awe, and
hesitated to go too close. Although still wet from the morning
dew, the grass was inviting; I sat and stared at the buildings and
imagined myself entering one of them, sitting in a neat row of
seats, and intensely concentrating on the inspiring words of a
kind, elderly professor full of great wisdom and knowledge.
After my classes, I would sit in a cheerful library and do my
lessons. Then there would be time for malts with a group of
friends and lots of talk about the books we were reading. After
four years of this, I would march down an aisle dressed in a black
cap and gown, and then—the world would be open to me.

"Hey you! Can't you read? The sign says, keep off the grass."

I was awakened from my daydream and jumped up to find a
crowd of students stopping to laugh at me on their way down the
cobbled walk towards the ivy-covered buildings.

Smoothing my hair and rumpled dress, I decided to follow
them and found myself in an old building which smelled of
sulphur. The crowd soon disappeared into classrooms, and I
wandered down the hallway feeling like a trespasser.

"May I help you?" a voice said, startling me as I rounded a
corner and met a man in a white lab coat.

"Are you looking for a room?" he continued.

"No. No thank you," I mumbled, trying to escape his eyes and
any more questions he might ask.

I hurried out of the building and into another just as the bell
rang, and students came out of the classes and rushed past me.
Their arms were full of books, and the girls were wearing expensive looking skirts and sweaters, even though the weather was
still warm. I felt naked and out of place in my thin, cotton dress,
barefoot sandals, and empty arms. It was with a sigh of relief that
I hurried away from the ivy-covered buildings, and the eyes that
asked what I had wanted there. When I entered the Greyhound
bus depot, I felt almost at home.

Sitting in the back of another bus that smelled of antiseptic this time, along with the usual gas fumes, I began to feel nauseated. I was overcome with self-pity, and my mind kept returning to the students—so secure looking, so sure of what they were doing—and to the college which represented another world I did not know how to enter. I wanted to cry because I, too, was not one of the fortunate ones receiving an education. But stiffening myself, I rationalized, what did these sheltered children know of life? They read about it while their parents paid the bills. I had something they didn't. I was free, on my own, and living. And had I not dreamed of becoming a poet? I must know life to write about it. And life again held a promise somewhere in the unknown future.

On arriving in Newburg, I realized I hadn't eaten all day. On the corner was a restaurant and I walked towards it. A sign in the window, "Waitress Wanted," vaguely caught my attention. It was a small restaurant, five booths, and about a dozen stools at the counter. On the large mirror facing the counter was a sign which stated, "This is a Grade B restaurant." Over the writing was some type of seal. I was later to find out the State rated all eating establishments by A, B, or C, and the owner was very proud of his B rating, the only one in town.

There was no one inside when I entered. I heard the sound of dishes rattling from within the kitchen, and soon a heavy-set, red-faced man, wiping his hands on a long white apron, appeared and asked, "What will you have?"

"Hamburger and coffee," I answered without looking at a menu.

He poured the coffee into a heavy brown mug and slid a clean-looking pitcher of cream in front of me, then withdrew to the kitchen where I heard the sound of meat sizzling on a grill.

The hamburger was good, and I felt better after eating it. The man had been in the kitchen all the time I was eating, and now he returned. "Anything else?" he asked.

Surprising myself, I smiled and said, "Yes. I'm looking for a job."

Thus began my nine-month employment with the Hiway Cafe. It was fun at first. I'd been lonely all summer, and I soon found that the truckers who stopped here were looking as much for conversation as for the two or three cups of coffee they drank. With the tips, I made more money than previously, received two meals a day, and didn't have a long bus ride each day.

I began buying books again and also found an old typewriter in a second-hand store. Many of the keys stuck, but it worked after a fashion. I now spent my time in the evening attempting to write poems, most of which were thrown in the wastebasket, but some I carefully kept in a black binder. I was working the early morning shift, six a.m. to two p.m., which gave me ample time for writing, reading, daydreaming, and sleeping.

At the restaurant I became acquainted with the truckers, loggers, and mill workers of the town, and joked with them as I served coffee and pie. After a few weeks, on one particularly bright autumn day when the leaves were falling and the air showed signs of changing to chill winter, one of the truck drivers asked if I would like to accompany him on his run when I finished working.

The cab of the truck was high and difficult to get into with a dress on. The driver laughed in a friendly way as he helped me in. As I straightened myself on the hard leather seat, and my friend started the engine and went through the business of shifting many gears, I had the same feeling I had experienced as a child on my first ride on the roller coaster. We began bouncing down the road, and I was impressed by how easy the driver sat in his place, and very self-conscious of my breasts in the tight fitting waitress uniform heaving up and down. I was hoping he wouldn't notice, and annoyed that he did, for with the skill of his profession he seemed to have little need for watching the road.

We drove a few miles until we came to a large open shed at the edge of a river. The driver slowly entered the shed, shut off his engine, and the bed of the truck was raised and the logs forced out one by one. We sat in the cab while the truck heaved and shook in delivering its load of newly cut brown logs to the river where they would float down to the mill. The workers laughed good-naturedly at my excitement watching this process. When it was finished and we drove back down the road faster now with the weight of the logs gone, my friend asked if I would like to go to Jake's.

"Who's Jake?" I asked.

He seemed to think this was enormously funny and almost before he was through laughing we were at Jake's.

Jake, I discovered, was a balding, cheerful person, who owned one of the local taverns. As we walked in Jake grinned at my friend and said, "Hey Tom! Long time no see."

"I've been on a long haul," Tom answered and steered me towards the bar.

Jake shoved two glasses of foamy tap beer towards us and smiled at me. "Who's the girl, Tom?"

"Julie. Jake." Tom nodded. "She's the new waitress at the Hiway."

"How long have you been in town?" Jake asked.

"Four months," I answered while nervously toying with the glass of beer in front of me. I was underage, and while I had drunk beer at high school parties, I'd never been in a tavern.

"It's a great town," Jake continued, "if you don't let it get you down."

I wondered what he meant by that, but as he and Tom both laughed, I joined them.

From the other end of the bar came a shout, "Hey Jake! Fill 'em up." And he left us alone.

Tom's friendly smile and his "Here's to you," as he tapped his glass against mine made me relax, and I tipped the glass, swallowing the amber liquid which tickled my nose.

We stayed all afternoon and most of the evening. I soon forgot how many glasses of beer I drank. I couldn't remember when I had last felt so good. Many of the truckers and loggers I knew from the restaurant were there, and they all seemed to envy Tom, which made me feel very important. We slid wooden discs back and forth on the long shuffleboard table part of the evening, and to my surprise I found that I was quite good at it. Jake was like an admiring father when I won. With each glass of beer, the tavern became more charming, Tom more handsome, and my new friends great people. It was with dismay that I remembered my job at six a.m.

That was my first of many nights at one of the Newburg taverns. No one ever asked where I was from, or why I came to this town, or how old I was. I was just there, and accepted. I was "Julie, the waitress at the Hiway," and at first Tom's girl, and then an available, single girl. I grew to know the people of this town. It was winter now, and with the heavy rains the mill work was at a minimum. Only a few people had jobs, and thus the men had more leisure time to spend in the taverns. Unemployment compensation lasted for twenty weeks, and when that ran out some had relatives they could move in with. There was always welfare if need be, and at least there was always someone in the tavern who would buy them a couple of beers. Slowly I became aware of life under the surface of the fun and laughs in the taverns. I began to see the gossip, the bickerings, the extra-marital affairs, and the Saturday night brawls that often turned into bloody fist-fights. I was a part of the town by this time—and yet I lived apart from it. I still considered myself a poet, al-though my old typewriter was being used very little now. I want-ed more than this town had to offer, but I didn't know where or how to find it.

Christmas came. I went to work as usual at six a.m. because the restaurant stayed open for the men who relied on it for breakfast. After work I returned home to have Christmas dinner with my aunt. She had cooked a chicken with mashed potatoes and gravy and opened green peas and cranberry sauce from the dark cellar where she kept her home-preserved foods. For des-sert we had raisin pie and coffee. After helping her with the dishes, we exchanged gifts in the cold living-room, and I thanked her for the sweater she gave me and immediately put it on. My aunt then settled herself on the sofa with her hand-knit shawl draped over her knees and proceeded to read the *Daily Word*, a small metaphysical magazine that was always at her side. I sat with her and read the evening newspaper. When my aunt turned on the six o'clock news on her table radio, I went to my room and began pacing the floor. Finally, I said to hell with it, put on a coat, and walked up to Jake's.

The tavern was crowded and a small green tree with red tinsel ropes and red and silver balls sat on the bar. Across the wide mirror behind the bar was scrawled "Merry Xmas," and holly leaves bordered it all. A sprig of mistletoe hung from the ceiling and Jake greeted me with a kiss and a "Merry Christmas Julie girl."

It was three o'clock in the morning when I arrived home. The old chestnut clock on the living room mantle was striking the hour as I tiptoed across the room and down the dark hallway past my aunt's door. Entering my room, I quietly shut the door behind me and collapsed on the bed. Feeling that I had hardly closed my eyes when the alarm clock rang, I reluctantly forced my attention to another day's work at the restaurant.

That was the beginning of many nights coming home early in the morning, going to work groggy-eyed and shaky, sleeping a few hours in the afternoon, and then back to the taverns. I seldom saw my aunt, and, when I did, her cold eyes and tightly-closed lips revealed the thoughts she never said to me. I didn't care. I no longer cared about anything except escape. To escape from the long, tedious mornings wiping counters and serving plates full of nauseous bacon and eggs. To escape from the howling wind, the beating rain and the endless mud which caked around the stools where the men in drab work clothes idly sat warming their hands on mugs of steaming coffee. When the first morning rush was over, I filled sugar bowls and cream pitchers, and dreamed of spring and leaving this town. My mind would wander to pictures I'd seen of New York and San Francisco, and I would imagine myself in a cozy room made warm by an open fire, lying on a thick carpet, surrounded by music and books, with gay, intelligent friends coming and going.

"Hey, Julie, get busy on the ketchup bottles," or "C'mon, Sis, I need help with these dishes before the noon rush," always jolted me back to reality.

I left the cafe each day with a determination to find something better in life than Jake's Tavern. Then, each evening, I would awaken from my afternoon sleep to the acrid smell of moth balls from the winter blankets on my bed and stare at the lifeless walls of my room and the stiff curtains now heavy with winter dust. The four pictures would again summon my attention. Jesus at the Last Supper had little meaning for me. He was aloof and sad looking, and I couldn't identify with him. I began to detest that picture, for its presence on my wall was a reproach much like my aunt's tight lips and unspoken words. I had more feeling for the shepherd who was alone and outside in the chill autumn air. I, too, was alone and cold, and I shivered as I thought of winter descending on this man and his flock. The sleeping baby all wrapped in blue once made me cry, but I didn't know why. My great uncle with the rakish eyes was a further reproach. He was so alive and young in that picture. Like a lie he looked at me. A lie of life existing in rakish eyes that were no more. Had he ever lain in this room and wondered what life was all about? I wanted to ask my aunt about him, but I never did. My reveries always changed to anger. I would then pace my room damning them all. Damn my aunt and this cold empty house, I would mutter. Damn the uncle I had never seen. Damn the Lord Jesus, the baby, and even the cold, lonely shepherd. And especially damn the rakish eyes that were no more. After this, I would once again end up at Jake's seeking refuge in the foaming, bitter tap-beer and the warmth of the tavern heater I clung to all through that long winter.

Before spring arrived I had a plan. I was going to leave Newburg. I was saving ten dollars a week, half my weekly pay, and my goal was a hundred dollars. With that much, I could surely escape, although to where I was never sure. New York City was my big dream, and I thought of going there by degrees. I would travel to Salt Lake City, or maybe Denver, and then work until I had enough money to go further, and eventually I'd reach New York. Time passed with this dream in my mind, which I never told to anyone.

Finally, a warm sunny day in late May arrived, and I withdrew my carefully saved money from the bank.

"Do you want it in tens or twenties, Miss?" the teller inquired.

I self-consciously asked if I could have a hundred dollar bill. The teller gave me a strange look, but handed me a crisp, green bill from deep within a drawer. It had Benjamin Franklin's picture on it, and it was beautiful. I fondled it caressingly when I was back home in my room. Here was my escape. But with the coming of spring, my plans had changed. I had fallen in love with one of the men who worked in the woods. He was strong, and good, and gentle, and on Saturday we were going to get married.

After a three-day, lakeside honeymoon, we rented an old garage that had been turned into a two-room house. There was a combination living room-bedroom upstairs, and a kitchen and bath downstairs. It was furnished with a double bed, a chest of drawers, a drop-leaf table and two chairs, and a hideous, black, wood-burning stove we laughingly called, "the monster." The woods were humming with work now, and my husband left early in the morning and returned late at night. I quit my job at the cafe, and spent my days contentedly painting the old furniture, sewing curtains for the bare windows, and learning to cook on the monstrous stove. In the evenings, I would read aloud from my books of poetry while my husband lay beside me listening to the words.

Three weeks went by in this fashion until one morning I was cleaning the kitchen floor a few hours after he'd left for work, and there was a knock at the door, and I looked up in surprise to see his father and mother. They told me there had been an accident in the woods. He was killed. I wanted to cry and couldn't, for sudden death is never really believable. I wanted to see for myself, but the mortician said, "No, for these accident cases are so messy." It was only when I saw his empty boots and the uneaten lunch I had packed that morning that the reality of death hit me, and I was able to cry.

After the funeral, as I, a nineteen-year-old widow, stood on another threshold of life, I was finally able to leave this depressed, distressed, small western town of seasonal employment and state compensation. How easy it was after all—even without the dream and the hundred dollars. I just bought a bus ticket and left.

Yellow Bird

"Hello."

"I have a collect call for a Mr. James Hernández from Mary Taylor."

"This is he."

"Will you accept the charges?"

"Yes."

"Go ahead."

"Jimmy?"

"Yes."

"I'm sorry I couldn't talk to you last time."

"So was I."

"I was scared. I'm still scared."

"I know."

"It's been sixteen years."

"A long time."

"God! Are we that old?"

"I guess we are."

"You've been O.K.?"

"I am now. And I hear you're becoming a teacher and happy and all. I'm glad you've done so well."

"Well . . . I don't know about that."

"What do you mean?"

"Oh, forget it. I want to talk about Carol."

"I wrote to her and asked her to visit us."

"I know. I read the letter."

"Oh."

"Jimmy?"

"Yes. Why are you crying?"

"She has to leave the nest."

"What do you mean?"

"It hurts, Jimmy. I'm scared, and she's even more scared. Help me."

"What can I do?"

"I've never said those words before."

"What?"

"Help me."

"I know."

"Do you remember her?"

"Of course I do. Our Yellow Bird."

"Funny you should say that. That's the day I remember the most. Her yellow dress and wispy yellow hair and we stood her on the coffee table—that crazy maple cobbler's bench we couldn't afford—and you didn't have a job and we waited for the donut truck every day, and we ground our own coffee beans, and . . ."

"Stop crying, Mary!"

"That was the day she walked for the first time. In that yellow dress, and you called her Yellow Bird."

"Stop crying!"

"Women need to cry—I used to try and tell you. You left a few months after that."

"I was sick, Mary. And I didn't want to go back to the hospital. I had to leave."

"I understand that now. I want you to see her."

"That would make me very happy."

"She's afraid to see you, Jimmy."

"Because of . . ."

"No. Maybe partly. But that's not the real reason."

"What is?"

"She's afraid of men, and she's young, and very insecure and mixed up right now."

"That can be normal."

"She needs a man to be good to her."

"She had Wayne."

"It was all a lie, Jimmy. I lied—especially to your mother."

"I don't understand."

"My marriage. It was no good. It hurt her. And now the divorce has hurt even more."

"But my mother sent pictures and always said how well off all of you were. She told me to stay away."

"I know. He was a good provider."

"And I never was."

"That's right. And you left. So I married him."

"We were crazy kids."

"Weren't we."

"But we had fun, didn't we?"

"Yes."

"We really did."

"And now you're married after all these years. I read your letter."

"What can I do, Mary?"

"She graduates from High School this month. I'd like you to come."

"I will."

"There's something else, Jimmy."

"What?"

"She just had an abortion."

"What! Is she alright?"

"Cool it. She's O.K. But she's still hurt and scared."

"How in the hell did that happen? Who is the guy?"

"It doesn't matter now. It's very common today. Not like when we were young. What matters is her future."

"What does she want? How can I help her?"

"There's one way."

"What is it?"

"She has to leave the nest, and she's afraid, and doesn't want to go one minute, and threatens to run away the next. I'm worried about her. Everything I try to do seems wrong."

"I don't even know her. What can I do?"

"Just be around, Jimmy. Let her meet her father."

"What good will that do?"

"If her wings fail, maybe you can catch her."

"You're crying again!"

"Goodbye, Jimmy. I can't talk anymore."

"I love you, Mary. I always did."

"I know that now. For God's sake, hang up."

Smile

I remember that evening, and I know now there was more to it than the growing pains. "She'll see things differently in a few weeks," friends and counselors had told me. But she didn't. Friends and counselors were wrong, and now all I can do is tell a little of her story, and how I learned how to smile.

We were living in Government Housing then, and I was being aided, or rehabilitated, to become a self-sufficient, working mother. I was happy most of the time then, freer and gayer after the divorce, in spite of—well, I forget the in-spite-ofs now. But I do remember:

"Where do you find the will to live, Mother?" She had asked me that a few weeks earlier.

"I'm leaving, Mom; I can't take it any longer." The year before my son had told me that.

"Whenever I think of you, all I can see is your smile": my youngest daughter had told me this during that week.

My answers? I had none. I couldn't tell my daughter to turn to God, because I had never known him. I told my son I understood. I smiled at my youngest daughter. Then I wondered about that smile. Somewhere along the way I had adopted the motto, "When in doubt, smile." It had gotten me through many a difficult situation. Only recently had I begun to re-evaluate the effectiveness of this. I was beginning to realize finally, perhaps too late, that smiles do not break down the walls that separate us from the unfulfilled promises life holds up to keep hope alive.

Before that remembered evening, she had sat in a chair every night for days staring at nothing. I could stand it no longer. The tensions and fighting had been growing worse, but now the silence was unbearable.

"What *is* wrong with you, Kathy?" I tried to hide my irritation. If only she'd try. If only she'd listen.

"I don't think I better tell you now because I know you have exams coming up." The innocent look didn't hide the hostility in her voice.

It took me three days to reach a decision after she told me her problem. I needed it over as quickly as possible, then. I came home early on that remembered evening, although the woman our social worker sent to stay with the children while I was at school was still there. She was a kind woman, and I needed her.

Kathy looked up at me when I entered the apartment. "Rob called." That was all she said. Her eyes were hard and cold. Was this my daughter?

"Yes?" I questioned. Rob was her father, and she had said she hated him. I had hated him once, but it was over now.

"I'm not going with him," she said to me.

"It's your father or Juvenile Hall." Oh, God, where was the love we used to have?

Mrs. Martínez spoke with her for a long while, showing her the advantages her father could offer her. She didn't listen.

"I won't go," she repeated.

Rob called four times, shouting in his usual way. "What have you done to her? What do you mean beyond control? Fuck those psychologists! You dirty bitch! If you had done what *I* told you. A case of neglect." I agreed on that point.

Kathy refused to speak with him. Mrs. Martínez gave up. I called the police as I had been instructed. Kathy sat in a chair smoking one cigarette after another defiantly staring at me. This had gone on for months, but I had waited and worked and hoped for a change.

A loud banging came from the apartment below us. "We're here for an uncontrollable juvenile."

Mrs. Martínez threw up her hands and went out onto the landing of our four-plex. I groaned to myself but never moved a muscle.

After muttering something about the apartment number, the officer turned to Kathy with a stupid grin and asked me to explain in what manner she was beyond control.

My voice was calm and firm and reasonable. I was almost smiling. "She refuses to obey and has been physically fighting with me. She won't attend school. She had an abortion two months ago, and she claims to be pregnant again."

She threw the package of cigarettes at me as she left with the officer. Does growing up have to be this painful was all I could think. I was alone, in the dark, in the same position as when she left, an hour later when the phone rang. She had relented and agreed to go with her father. They needed my permission.

I stopped smiling after that. Learning to cry was difficult. Learning how to use the tears was even more difficult. But I did learn how to save my smiles for very special occasions.

Happy Hour

It was an extra hot Friday in early August with the long summer's discouragement of "still no work" behind me until Monday, the admission that $30.18 would never stretch until September floating above me, and the knowledge of Dave sitting alone in a hotel room probably broker than I, still too frustrating for me to comprehend. I had just walked into this 12 × 20 foot room I temporarily called home when the phone rang. I knew who it was before I answered, but then maybe— maybe—these fragile maybes I had been living with.

"Hi! Whatcha doing?" It was Betsy. Maybe someday I'd be wrong.

"Wanta meet me over at Las Brisas?" She never waited for an answer to her questions, and her voice was slightly slurred from the Vodka I had a mental picture of her sitting on her sofa sipping. "If we leave now," she continued, "we can be there by six and there will still be an hour of Happy Hour left. They bring out more food at 6:15, and you know how I love to eat." She laughed. "Beats cooking in this weather also. But I can only afford one drink. A double and all we can eat for a dollar. Wanta go?"

"O.K. I'll meet you out front at six." I hung up and sat by the phone feeling a complete lack of enthusiasm. Happy Hour! I had gone twice before and never felt happy. I love music and dancing, but that doesn't begin until 9:00, and Betsy never makes it that long. I stared around the room, and all I could see were papers. Jobs, jobs, jobs that I didn't get. Re-typed resumés, application forms, cover letters, brochures. By their side were the notes, notes, and more notes for the incomplete seminar paper that still wasn't done. And it's August now. The perspiration was already running down my face. I rose and went towards the bathroom with a firmer feeling. Anything was better than staying here tonight. Spend a dollar and be happy. At least I'd be cool.

I arrived at Las Brisas five minutes before Betsy. She parked her car and walked towards me. She had on a conservative pant-suit and her short-hair blonde wig. "Hey," she said, laughingly, as we walked towards the entrance to the bar, "you look like a hippy."

"Thanks," I snarled.

"I meant it as a compliment," she snapped back.

"O.K. I apologize. I'm just feeling hot and tired, and a little shitty." We both laughed now, but I was too aware of the contrast between us. Happy Hour and why not? I had told myself as I hastily dressed. So hot, and I had thrown on a thin cotton back-less, braless, red and white check dress, leather sandals, grabbed my fringed import handbag, and ran a comb through my hair, letting it fall loosely without arrangement.

We found two stools at the far end of the bar and sat down. It was crowded, and the hum of conversations made it difficult to hear Betsy. "We'll never get a waitress, and besides we can save a quarter by not tipping," she was fairly shouting at me.

"O.K." The message was reaching me now and I gave her a dollar. She took off to get our drinks and food. I sat there and looked at the small groups of sophisticated-looking people, won-dered what I was doing here, and wondered once again why Betsy and I were friends when we had so little in common. It was crowded and air conditioned. I began to relax and feel some of the tenseness leave me. The cool air was reaching me, and the conversational hum began to sound like soft music. When Betsy returned with two tall tequila sunrises and two plates full of chicken, shrimp and cocktail sized tacos, I knew why we were friends.

Iced drinks are wonderful things. I stared into my now half-empty glass. "I wonder who invented ice?"

"What?" Betsy asked.

"Who invented ice?"

"The bartender."

That conversation was over. I stared deeper into my drink and laughed. Betsy looked at me now.

"What's so funny?"

"Not even Shakespeare could sit in a hot room alone and write on a night like this," I answered.

She gave me a quizzical look and changed the subject. "I think those two guys at that corner are looking at us."

I was still staring into my drink when two fresh drinks arrived in front of us. "I was right," Betsy gloated. She nudged me. "We'll have to thank them."

I looked around and saw two men who tipped their drinks at us and smiled. I smiled a thank you back. Betsy was excited. "Shall we ask them to join us?"

Without waiting for an answer from me, Betsy had gone to their table and I could see her smiling and talking. She returned to me, and we then moved ourselves to the men's table. Happy Hour, I thought, why must I be feeling so negative, and when will I look at a man and not compare him with Dave?

Another round of drinks was placed on the table. Betsy was laughing at a joke. Why didn't I join? Why didn't I laugh? Why were the faces one big blur?

"Have you heard this one?"

"Whatsa matter with your friend?"

"You're just what I've been waiting for. Umm! Umm!"

"Cheer up the world won't end until tomorrow."

"I've got a bottle of tequila just up from old Mex, lemons hanging on the tree, and two steaks waiting on the grill."

Betsy and the man next to her were gone. I felt a hand on my leg and a voice saying, "You'd be a real looker if you didn't take life so serious."

The summer exploded in me. I fought back tears and ran to a phone booth in the lobby.

"Extension 230, please," I said to the hotel clerk.

"Hello." It was Dave's voice. My mind blanked, and I dropped the receiver.

Home. Go home. Have coffee and sit up all night and work on the Shakespeare paper. That's all that matters now. That's my love. Drive slow. Summer exploding. Take it easy. Dave used to tell me that. Know this freeway so well. Make it in ten minutes, he'd say. Can drive it in my sleep. 28th St. No. Swerve. Don't live there anymore. Two years hard to forget. Next exit. My lonely barrack home. Go slow. Oh, no! Flashing red light behind me. Where do I stop. Off the ramp. It's O.K. Four blocks home.

The siren, like Dave's voice on the phone, brought me to a

sudden stop. The officer approached. It's O.K. I was stopped once before. I'm almost home. Be cool, cooperative, respectful.

"Yes, I was weaving. I swerved. I was going slow. I was looking for the right exit. Yes, I was drinking. I was with a friend. Where? A place cross town."

His face was a blur like the man in the bar. I reached inside my bag for my license.

"I'll take that," he said, and began searching my bag. "So you are taking pills, too."

"No. That's a prescription I got today and forgot to take out." Confusion was sobering me now.

"And you're a student. Huh, lady?" he continued, "And what do you study in that dress? Why isn't a ring on your finger, instead of this?" He fingered the chain around my neck where I wore the spoon ring Dave had made.

"Stop! You have no right to touch me."

"Give me your keys."

"No."

"Give me your keys." He was loud and held my left arm.

"No," I answered still, but fear was now weakening my voice.

He opened the car door, undid my seat belt, pushed me across the seat and drove the car around the corner to a side street where he parked it.

"Give me your arms," he demanded.

"No." I resisted in spite of fear, but my arms were soon tightly behind me, and secured in steel handcuffs. The officer was gone. I looked up and saw a crowd of people on the sidewalk. Anger and sympathy were in their faces. Police cars were not a welcome sight in this neighborhood. If I could reach the crowd I'd be O.K. I fought the handcuffs trying to reach the door handle before the officer returned. I couldn't make it. I shouted, "Help me. Help me." The faces understood, but they didn't move.

Another police car arrived. I was removed from my car and placed in the officer's car. He took off up the freeway ramp, going fast. He wanted to talk. "So you're a student. So what do you study? So what good will it do you? Why don't you have a man? Do you know where we are going?"

I answered him in monosyllables with only the increasing pain of the steel handcuffs my focus point in reality. It was dark now, and the car finally stopped. My door was opened, and I was led into a building. It was a small, stark room with a table and chairs and a few police officers standing around. I was pushed into a chair and the handcuffs unlocked. Before I could rub my aching wrists or straighten my arms, I was held by two policemen and papers were placed before me to sign. I signed without reading them. A needle was in my arm and I watched a tube filling with blood. My blood. "Now what?" I finally spoke.

"I'm taking you to the women's detention center," the officer answered.

"No," I cried out in final desperation, "That's not necessary."

"A student," he laughed.

He took me for another ride and led me into a large, strange building. There were buzzers and doors that opened, and finally an entrance hall with two young girls, another policeman, an iron mesh screen with matrons, counters, and office space behind it. He gave my handbag to the matron behind the screen. I was freed of the handcuffs at last. Again, there was no time to rub my arms. I was ordered to remove my jewelry. A watch. Pierced earrings. The chain and ring around my neck. They were sealed in an envelope. He handed me papers to sign, long and detailed. I asked for my glasses, they were in my bag, and this time I wanted to see what I was signing.

The officer gave me a last angry look and took the papers from me. He signed them, said "Too drunk," as he handed them to the matron, and he left.

I began to feel less fear and more anger now that he was gone. One of the young girls was crying and refused to remove her wedding ring. I spoke up. "You could at least let her have that. A wedding ring is sacred."

Another buzzer and I was pushed into the inner chamber. Was it the prison? A matron held my arm firmly and led me down a hall into a small square empty room where she stood at the door demanding that I remove all my clothing. She watched while I removed the flimsy braless dress, sandals, and red bikini undies. She then ordered me to face the wall and place my palms against it while I squatted and then rose three times. By the third time I had learned what hatred was. The matron then threw me a pair of flour sack pajamas. We watched each other as I dressed. She was dressed in a green cord pantsuit, and her flawless hair was a wig not too different from Betsy's. Her eyes were cold and filled with contempt. I wanted to ask her if she was wearing white cotton undies.

She gripped my arm again and led me back into the hallway where I stood before a counter. The pajamas didn't fit and I tried to hold the top together to cover my breasts. My feet were bare, and the cold of the cement floor was causing me to shiver. Another matron came forward with another paper for me to sign. Two dimes had been taken from my belongings, and I had to sign for them. I was informed of my rights.

"You have been arrested on a criminal charge under section VC23102A. You are allowed two phone calls. Do you wish to make them?"

My anger had subsided, and I was too aware of the cloth pajamas, my bare feet, and the pain of the handcuffs. I felt like a young school girl, harshly brought before the class, unprepared for her lesson, and severely reprimanded, while also unaware of what the consequences could be.

"What is VC23102A?" I asked. "Who do I call? How do I get out of here?"

"Drunk driving. $300 bail, or get a bondsman." The hand on my arm tightened. I was pushed towards the phone.

"You are not allowed to dial. Give me the name and the number."

I was feeling hysterical now, and who could I call? A yellow page bondsman? Legal Aid? It was eleven p.m. on a Friday night. One of my professors? Maybe the woman's center? Why is August so far from May? My doctor? I saw him today and he was concerned about me. He gave me medication for my blood pressure.

The matron called. I wasn't allowed to touch the phone. Confusion, and no, I don't know a lawyer and a too-quick goodbye.

There was no one else but Dave. I gave the matron his number. She held the receiver while I shouted into it. "I'm in jail! Yes, I'm hysterical. Get me out of here. I'll do anything."

"I won't have any money until Monday," was all he said.

"Well, do something," I cried. The matron hung up the phone.

She then pushed me across the hall to another room and said, "We have to search you." Before I could even think, "What is there left to search," she pushed me heavily, and I fell to the floor. The door shut and I was alone. Slowly the confusion began to clear. I stood up and tried the door. It was locked. There was a window. I looked out. The two matrons stood next to the counter and the telephone. They were drinking coffee. I saw a sink then and paper towels and a jar of instant coffee. A desk covered with papers was in the corner and a clock was above it. It was 11:03. A long bench was in front of my window. Three young women sat on the bench. They had on pajamas like mine and rubber thongs on their feet, and they were drinking coffee and smoking cigarettes. I wanted to sit in the hall with coffee and cigarettes and someone to talk to and understand this confused mess. I made motions to the matrons. I was ignored. I beat on the window until I realized it was hopeless.

I turned within then and surveyed my room. Approximately 8 × 10 feet square. There was a toilet in the corner, a roll of paper, two army blankets on the floor, and that was all. Be grateful for the window, but how I hated it later when I had to use the toilet. Hold on to myself and avoid panic at all costs. Always had a fear of confinement. Sit. Maintain my dignity. I sat cross-legged with one blanket under me and the other one over my shoulders. Was it really hot outside? Sit. They have to let me out eventually. Calm and dignity. Avoid all else. I could see the large clock from where I sat. An hour went by. Must let them know I am still here and in need. Beat on the window again. Gain attention. They saw me and still ignored me. I sat again. I rubbed my legs to keep warm. I remembered old friends who were involved in the civil rights of the early sixties. They had sat in a hot jail, also empty of provisions, and had sang. I imagined they were with me. I sang, "We Shall Overcome." Another hour went by. Must try again. Matter of principle now. Use the blanket to protect my arm. Keep beating on that window. They looked at me with cold anger in their eyes. Enough. Don't tire self. I laid down and rested for a half hour. Eventually. Have to let me out eventually. I remembered studying Baldwin's novel and the discussion we had about Richard's suicide after being in prison. I was feeling it. This destruction of the human spirit. No. We shall overcome. Sit. Fight. I am a woman. I need to feel my earrings. I need to dangle the chain around my neck. I need to brush my hair. I need Kleenex. Not that harsh toilet paper. More hours. The window every hour. Do not hope. Act and wait. It was eight a.m. and the new shift was coming on duty. I had been in here since eleven p.m. I stood at the window so they could see me. I watched them go about their work. The prisoners were dressed in knee-length, sleeveless muumuus. They were led into breakfast. The matrons made motions to me that I didn't understand. I held my head high. Maintain dignity and self respect now at all costs. It was nine o'clock. I sat back down. There was a hot bath at home. A Shakespeare paper waiting to be done. Eventually would come. Eventually.

The Woes of a Single Woman and Her Car

I'm feeling very angry at Car today and know it is time to force a showdown with her. She has let me down one time too many.

I walk out to look at her parked in the mud of the back lot. How sad and beat she looks. Well—she has to face reality someday and grow up just like everyone else. Don't be easy on her. Remember this is for her own good.

"Hey, Car," I shout.

She doesn't answer. She's still clinging to her pride. I know her ways.

"Car," I shout again, "know what? You are a fucking creep, that's what. Here you sit in the mud and don't do a good-God-damn thing to help yourself. Don't you know that your water pump is broken, and your front end is cracked and crooked, and your tires are bald, and God only knows what else is wrong with you? And you have the gall to sit here in plain sight of everyone, and even dare to look a little sassy at times, also.

"Jesus, you make me sick, Car. Do you really think someone is just gonna' come along and rescue you? You gotta' help yourself—you creep."

I kick her back bumper to emphasize my point. Then I continue.

"You waiting for Prince Charming to come along, Car? Think he's gonna' ride into your life and replace your water pump or take you to the store and deck you out in new tires? Who the fuck you think you are, huh? Don't you know everyone has their problems? When you gonna' realize that and stop expecting others to do things for you? You're weak. Weak! Weak!"

With my increasing anger I kick away at her right front tire, the weakest one. It splits open and the air hisses at me. Car slumps to the right, settling more firmly into the mud.

I feel a little guilty now. Maybe I was too harsh on her—even if it was for her own good. After all, we *were* friends once.

"Car," I speak softer now, "nothing personal about this, O.K.? It's just that your helplessness frustrates me too much, and also you never do what I expect of you. Besides, you really do need to learn how to take better care of yourself and stop depending on others."

I sort of want to pat Car on her rear window now as I back away. "Well, Car," I say while leaving, "when you get yourself together, drop around. I got my own troubles, you know. Be seeing you."

I walk away now fully knowing the impotence of my anger. No matter how many times I have shouted at Car and have kicked her, she still refuses to move. I think I always knew she was lacking in character.

I wrap my old coat tighter around me now as I walk off into the January rain hoping today to find a sunset I can fade into. With luck I may also find a field of May flowers I can throw myself into the midst of and feel once again that never-never land where everything just is because it is with no need to ever question why.

The Bathetic Fallacy

It was late April with spring only now beginning to appear as
I dragged my graduate-student-scarred body out of bed and
down to Peanuts for an early breakfast and a few moments of
quiet.

Peanuts is a small cafe across the street from San José State
University. The long winter months had found me huddled at a
back table listening to the rain and the drone of students' conversations while I studied for my comprehensive examinations.
Now, all the postponed seminar papers were due. Five papers in
five weeks. If spring were surely coming, I, for one, had no time
to herald her.

Thus, I was sitting with my coffee and my 99¢ Special, jotting
notes on research I needed to pursue at the library that day,
when three strangers entered the cafe.

Well, I said to myself, at Peanuts, at 7:30 a.m., in late April,
most anything could happen. I watched as the strangers paid for
tea and sat at a table next to me. They carefully measured sugar
into their styrofoam cups and swished a Lipton's bag back and
forth. At first I thought they were Hare-Krishnas, but a closer
look showed their sack cloth robes to be more of an off-white, not
yellow, and their hair was long, not shaved or ponytailed.

Research and work calls, I told myself at this point. I had not
time to ponder strangers. But damn! What were they? Buddhist
monks? Jesus disciples? Drama students had their private coffee
club, and philosophy majors never got up until noon. Could be
some freaked-out psych. students, but then I knew most of them.

Curiosity overcame me. "Please excuse me," I said leaning
forward towards their table, "but, would you mind telling me
what—uh—who, you—uh—represent?"

The brown-faced one who appeared to be their leader as he directed the movements of the sugar bowl, smiled at me and stood up.

"I'm Ethos," he stated. "I believe in the guiding principles of moral duty and obligation. I always consider ethics before acting."

Ooooh! These long winter months studying had really got to me. "Look," I stammered, "I'm sorry about this. I don't usually talk to strangers."

"That's logical," blurted out the second stranger as he stood. "I'm Logos. I believe in the divine wisdom of speech, reason, and the word."

"I'm an English major myself," I answered him, feeling more comfortable. "And who are you?" I asked the third stranger who had remained seated.

"That's Pathos," the first stranger answered.

"I can speak for myself," the seated one said as he also stood and looked at me. "I believe in the power of artistic expression to evoke pity and compassion," he told me. "I'm pathetic."

"I'm very sorry to hear that," I answered him, not knowing what else to say to this poor soul.

"Thank you. I'm pleased," he responded.

I couldn't let it end here, with his poor-soul eyes looking at me like a puppy in need of a good dog biscuit. "Look," I said reaching towards him, "I do a little writing myself. Have you tried an agent?"

Ethos spoke up next. "We highly respect age," he told me. "We have all studied under Socrates."

"Will you join us?" Logos invited me. Perhaps he saw my puzzled look.

"Thank you," I answered and moved to their table with my mind attempting to grasp this situation in every possible manner.

By now I assumed the strangers were guys, although you never know about Greeks. But I decided the masculine noun would be my best choice. "What are you guys doing in San José?" I asked.

"We came to help you," they answered in unison.

"Yeah?" I said. I hadn't completely ruled out the Jesus disciples *or* the Drama students.

They just sat there smiling at me and waiting for more of an answer.

"Me?" I asked, feeling the incredibility of the situation.

Ethos spoke up. "If you could look upon us as your guardian angels," he said, "then, how could we best aid you?"

This was too much to believe. Instead of the one angel of mercy I had prayed for, I'd gotten three Greek philosophers. Venus must have been in my ruling sign of Taurus that day.

"I really appreciate this," I answered, reaching for my notes. "Now, here are subjects to pursue in the card catalog, and be certain to avoid all books published prior to 1932, and then—"

"Wait . . . wait . . . wait, my dear," Logos said. "We must approach this is a very logical manner."

"No, Logos," Ethos took over, "We always begin by considering the ethics involved. Now, let's examine the real questions."

"If you are worried about using my library card," I spoke up. They weren't listening. Ethos and Logos were still debating the question. "Look guys," I almost shouted, "I just want to pass my classes."

"Of course," Pathos defended me. "You must remember the human issue. She is only a mere woman. Like Ismene."

Ordinarily I would have argued at this point, but I couldn't really expect these characters to understand the women's liberation movement. Besides, if it would get my library work done, then I'd consort with Greek chauvinists for a day. "Yes, I'm only a woman," I answered. "Do you guys know how to use the library?"

"Of course," Logos answered. "Human or not, that is where we must begin. We must approach the library in a logical manner."

I knew this guy was an English major. I *was* feeling better.

Ethos jumped up again. "That's old Logos for you. He still doesn't care about the *real* issue. When writing papers, the quality of what is said from honest convictions must precede all else. If not, then what does education mean? What does life mean? What does life after death mean? Without ethics we will be living in a world where all values are dead and life is reduced to nothingness."

God! I thought he was an old Greek and this guy was coming

on like Hemingway! I wondered if he had any wine in the sheep-skin flask hanging around his neck.

"Gentlemen, gentlemen," Pathos was loud now. "The only real issue is the human. This woman must pass her courses— which means papers."

"Ah yes—papers," Ethos had mellowed out and stared off nostalgically. "Like dear old Aristotle. Now if he were here."

Logos stamped his foot. "I thought you were so damned ethical. Now you have *plagiarism* on your mind."

"That's only human in a situation like this," insisted Pathos.

"The human! The human!" said Logos in a rage. "People like you would have all of us running through the woods like nymphs and fauns."

I grasped his arm. "How did you know? How much do you know?"

"Know what?" all three asked.

"That's one of the papers I must do," I answered, "Marvell's 'A Nymph Crying Over the Death of Her Faun'."

"If only Diana were here," said Pathos.

"Lot she'd know about the library," Logos answered.

"Your stinking logic spoils all our parties," Ethos cried.

"Now don't feel bad again, Ethos," Pathos said patting his head.

Oh dear. This was getting out of hand. Never lean on a Greek, my mother used to say.

"Ethos," I asked, "Could that by chance be wine in the flask hanging around your neck?"

He brightened.

"And, Logos," I asked, "Is that tube protruding from your robe a flute?"

He hugged me.

"Is there a meadow nearby?" Pathos asked.

The library was forgotten as we headed towards William's Street Park. I'll probably flunk out of school as I am relating this story; but, who can resist wine and flute playing, and running among the trees with people able to tell really good tales.

Bits & Pieces

1

This story is for you, Ken. I call it "Bits & Pieces" because that's all I ever had really. Bits & pieces of a life and bits & pieces of a man.

Maybe you will remember my Seventh St. apartment and the year I was a full-time graduate student living with my fifteen-year-old daughter Lisa, my Siamese cat, and my hopes of becoming a successful writer. You were a part of that year.

I wonder if you will remember how many times I had to run from you so I could find you. Maybe that's why all I have is bits & pieces.

2

It's May and I'm meeting Ken for lunch today, and I wonder why I'm seeing him again, but then, why not? I get in the car and so much is forgotten and too much remembered. I think about the story of O'Neill and the woman he loved, and I too want to say I want to spend every day of the rest of my life with you. I'm surprised when he heads up the freeway for San Francisco. We sit at that same outdoor cafe on the wharf where he took me shortly after we met. He does not remove his so very dark glasses and he says very little. I chatter, and then I feel slowly, then more strongly, how I am his little sparrow, pecking away at his crumbs, while he sits back amused, and sets traps for me, and then he holds me too tightly and bruises my wings.

That day we met was such an obvious trap as he paced the floor staring at me, and I could have looked away, but I didn't. When he sat at my table I thought perhaps we had met before, but we hadn't. We talked, and there were all the coincidences. Three hours later I was dressed in that crazy red and yellow striped silk skirt with the fringed belt, waiting to go out to dinner, and Lisa said maybe this is the boyfriend you've been waiting for, but I told her no, and laughed, but why did a part of me want to run? He arrived early. The freeway was slow and the dinner was long. We talked, and had we really known so many of the same people, and been in the same places for all these years? Twenty-four hours later he brought me home, and nothing like that has ever happened to me before then or since then.

3

Sitting in the park reading, waiting for him, and I look up and see him coming across that long expanse of grass from the other side. He walks slow and uncertain, and has that pouting look. He is wearing black boots, modest, zippered, not too shiny, white linen pants, slightly soiled, a brightly striped velveteen shirt, scoop-necked and sleeveless, so bold and reckless, and new glasses, gold framed, dark lenses, unable to see his eyes behind those lenses, those brooding eyes, vulnerable eyes, angry eyes.

We walk across the grass to the trees. He leans against a lone tree where there is no room for me. I stand there feeling weak, and with nothing to lean on. He pulls out a leather key case. It is new, and I feel an instant dislike of it. He has two joints inside. He lights one, and closes his eyes with that deep inhalation I have seen before. He reaches in his pocket and withdraws a silver peace sign with a red button, a holder for his joint.

I go forward and lean against him. It is easier now, the pressure of resistance gone. I feel neither warm nor cold, and I begin talking, talking, again; it is easier this way.

We lay on the grass with my head on his chest and I can feel his breathing. He is patting me, but he is not with me. He is with the sun, the trees, and the sky.

I remember that first day he brought me home and my heart was so firm and happy. "I feel good about you," I told him. He was strong and gentle then. This man is a stranger who frightens me, and I am clinging to a memory, not a man.

4

His cigarettes were on top of the chest in the hall, the remains of dinner sat on the table, and his bottle of Heinekens stood out, untouched.

I sat down slowly, drank my beer, then his, and tried to piece together what had happened. The phone rang, the music was loud, an old Aretha Franklin, and it was Jan on the phone.

"The loan. What's this about December 1? What bank? Your boyfriend is there? You have a long cord. Go in the other room."

"If you leave the room, I'm going," he said.

I went into the hall, half left, half there, wanting to satisfy both of them, confusion beginning. "I explained all this," I told Jan. "It's only a formality. What's the problem?"

He walked out. "He just left. He's angry because I'm on the phone."

"Run after him," she said.

"No," I answered. "That's his problem."

She kept talking, but I heard nothing. "Let me call you back," I told her, "I'm feeling upset."

He walked back in. "Where is my sweater?" he asked.

It was a special sweater. One he had let me keep. I didn't answer him. He was going through the drawers like Lisa did last spring when she was angry and insisted I had money I didn't have.

I was feeling strangely calm. "Why did you do that? She was co-signing for a loan. I need money by the end of the week."

"Where is my sweater?"

"I don't know," I answered him. I sat down. He left.

I stared at the bottles remembering. "She's a friend. Here's an $83 check for my tuition. She's co-signing for a loan on my loan. I'll have $2500 for my graduate year."

I took the phone off the hook, seeing his eyes, hearing her voice, remembering that day, weeks before I met him, Lisa and I had just moved in this apartment, and we were happy and proud. She came to visit. She borrowed something or other before we went out for the evening. She laughingly made a joke about borrowing from her "destitute friend."

"Don't use that word," I had shot out at her, but I was laughing also.

Now I sat here and felt what it was like to be "destitute." I had never felt it until now. I prepared for bed. I might be called tomorrow to do substitute teaching. I must earn money, first, and then think about school. I put the phone on the hook and went to sleep. It began ringing. I couldn't answer it. I couldn't talk. Not now. It rang again. When it stopped I took it off the hook. I had to sleep so I could work. I couldn't sleep. I wouldn't get a call to work with the phone not working. I put it back on the hook. It rang. I put it in the closet. It still rang. I couldn't sleep. By early morning I knew I was not able to work that day.

5

And only he knows the last day that happiness came from the bottom of my heart. And is January that far from June? How much closer is last August when I said, "Knowing where my heart is, regardless," and we sat on his bed fighting over a piece of ham, naked and laughing, and then he never made love to me because he was angry that I didn't put the orange juice away.

Such a strange man. He doesn't know how to be free and natural with his love. Like Aretha, I call out, "Don't you know, don't you know, don't you know, baby, I was the best thing you ever had!"

6

There was a loud knock at the door and I knew it was him, and I put the chain on the latch, and I stood behind the bookcase to the side of the door, and I then opened it.

"I don't want to see you."

"This is my friend José. You are embarrassing me in front of my friend."

I'm shaking and tears are in my eyes now as I say, "You are hurting me," and "read my letter."

"It's sealed. You're angry about the woman. Let me in."

"I'll call the police. Stop it." And he's pushing on the door and can easily break it like he did the screen door last summer.

"Meet José, and I'll leave."

His beige knit shirt and suede jacket and all six feet four inches still pressing on the door, and his eyes? No change, but what are they saying? And, "You are either with me all the way, or against me, and that's where it's at," and "Hello, José," and drowning his words, "That's shit, shit!"

"I'll go away and you'll never see me again. Let me in."

"That might be your loss and my gain."

"You lied to me."

"You never knew me."

"I wanted to be nice. My friend and I brought some wine. If you had any guts."

And tears down my face as he eases off and I shut the door. Sinking down crying—is this Ken?

At two a.m. the phone rang and I sat up and I looked at it and I reached for it and I touched it, but I didn't answer it.

7

After we had sat at that cafe. After we had sat at the ocean and he said, "Do you want me?" not knowing, not suspecting, that I wanted to rent a San Francisco apartment, not a motel. After he had made love to me—love which was all force and no control, love which was all aching and demanding and never satisfying—then he sat in a chair while I was on the bed drinking champagne, the wrappers from our hamburgers littering the table where I groped for an ashtray, and he slowly lit a joint, and he told me about the woman who was pregnant, and had refused an abortion, and had turned him in to the district attorney. I saw the avoidance in his eyes, and I felt the pain in mine, and I knew he didn't see it, and he would never know the love I had for him.

8

And he said, "Don't talk about love," so I didn't. And can I now go out like Dylan Thomas, not gentle into that good night, but "rage, rage, against the dying of the light?"

For Ken, too, was one of the "wild men who caught and sang the sun in flight, and learn, too late, they grieved it on its way."

9

Everything is packed except for these few belongings I must use tonight. The truck will be here at eight a.m. I sit for the last time at this old oak desk with my typewriter. I'll miss this desk. It, like too much of myself, will stay in this apartment. Look out tonight. Look out the window. I see the banana trees rustling. I see the large pink hibiscus flowers that were so much in bloom last summer. One is trying to crawl in the hole in the window. Such a large hole and I've lived with it all through the Spring months. My heart is broken like this dirty window I reach and touch here so close to my typewriter. Can it be mended for $40 or $50 like the window? My artist's apartment, I called it, with the dark beam ceilings, oriental rug, old-fashioned kitchen filled with wood cupboards, and this window. With the dreams, the doing, and the love. With my daughter, Lisa, with me, and then Ken came along, and the letter from New York arrived which said, if nothing else, that I was a writer. All the fragile maybe's. Ken saying I'd be famous some day, but he did nothing about it.

November came and I was standing in this room in my pink robe, like the flowers, with the news that Lisa was pregnant and her father had put her in a home for unwed mothers. My school loan was lost and I was three months behind on my rent. I had a notice that the utilities were being shut off the next day. My seminar report was due next week, and I hadn't yet read *Absalom, Absalom.* Ken had disappeared. I awoke in the morning, and like one of Hemingway's characters, I, too, knew my heart was broken, and I, too, knew, "great advice, try and take it some-time." Hemingway shot himself. All I did was throw an iron candle-holder through my window.

But when I am gone, now, will I remember little things? Will I see this window? My cat sitting in it? Ken on the stool singing to me? Lisa eating her cereal? Will the trees rustle? And no, I'll never again awaken to my pink flowers and to the bells coming from school. But, can this much sorrow be turned to strength?

10

And I now place one-half of my memories in a manila enve-lope to be mailed to you along with this story. The unopened letters of last summer. Paper wrapped sugar from that first night. A fortune, from a Chinese cookie, a week later. Directions to your apartment. Later directions to your desires, and I sat next to you, and wrote them down, also. A stick from the beach. A match cover. A motel receipt. The notes you left on my screen door. Our pictures. Our song, on a 45 r.p.m., and a dozen half finished poems.

The books are packed. I'm ready to leave. And every good existentalist knows that Godot isn't coming.

The Poster

It was late afternoon in the small office of the Bureau of Local Affairs. The day had turned unusually hot and oppressive for early May, and a large fan was whirring overhead. A short wiry man was nervously pacing the floor. "Five o'clock, and they're not here yet," he muttered and stared viciously at the ugly black telephone on his desk. As if in answer to this man's mumbling, the telephone rang loudly, and the man eagerly lunged towards it. "Hello," he shouted. "Jones, it's you! Where the hell are you? Never mind all that! Did you get the posters? Uh-huh, uh-huh," he kept muttering while looking at the large clock on the opposite wall whose black arrow-like hands had just jumped to the quarter hour.

"Well, how soon can you make it? No good, Jones. The rally starts at six-thirty sharp, and the Governor is counting on fifty of those posters for the parade. If we don't produce, it's the Arizona borax mines."

With this statement, a knock was heard at the door and a shout, "Peterson, are you there?" Without waiting for a reply, a tall man entered, followed by six elderly men each carrying large paper rolls.

The man on the telephone looked up and asked half-gleefully, half-anxiously, "The posters?"

"All fifty of them."

"Jones," he shouted back into the telephone, "we got them. Hurry over, and forget everything else."

Peterson, feeling assured of his comfortable and usually not so hectic government job and of not being sent to the Arizona mines, leaned back in his swivel chair while one of the posters was spread against the wall for his approval.

"Ah, beautiful, beautiful," he kept repeating, while closely scrutinizing the extra large poster that was to be displayed to the crowd that evening. It was made to imitate one of the old scenic checks from the Bank of Amerika. The branch bank printed on the check was Isla Vista at Goleta, Ca., which was the first bank to be completely burned down by the leaders of the Revolution. Red and yellow flames blazed across the check boldly depicting the burning building.

"Ah, beautiful, beautiful," again Peterson stated, and then with a sudden thought asked, "but are you sure it's an authentic reproduction? It's been fifty years."

At this the tall man pointed with pride at his six elderly companions. "Is it authentic, gentlemen?"

"Yes," they answered in unison.

Peterson had been too interested in the poster to notice the men before. Now he gave them a close look. They were all elderly, probably in their middle seventies, he thought, and quite well dressed. Could be retired students by their looks.

"Pete, meet California's six surviving Veterans of the Revolution. They were all at San José State University that glorious day of May 8, 1970 when the bombing started. These are our guest speakers for the rally."

Peterson was overwhelmed. He had met many important men through his work, but never one of the actual surviving revolutionaries. There were few people left who could even remember when it had started.

Another knock sounded at the door. It was opened, and a uniformed chauffeur appeared, who informed them that the limousine was ready to depart for the rally. Peterson hastily wrote a message for Jones and left with the men.

When they arrived at the State Capitol where the rally was scheduled, a crowd had gathered in front of the building and were seated quietly on folding chairs. The eight men walked onto the speakers' platform and were introduced to others. It was the eve of May 8, and all the heads of the State were expected to arrive. The chiefs of the Student's Bureau, the People's Police, and the League of Professors were already present, along with a few minor dignitaries.

The chief of the People's Police began explaining the plans for the evening and in which direction the parade would take place. As he was pointing down the main avenue from the Capitol, a rumbling noise became discernible and a large crowd of marchers rounded the corner and came into view.

"It's those radical bankers again," said the chief of the Student's Bureau.

The marchers were carrying banners that stated: Freedom, Equality, All Power for the People, Money for the People.

"Rabble rousers," shouted the chief of the Professor's League, "why do people listen to those scum."

"Call out the R.O.T.C.," the chief of the People's Police shouted to his aide. "We must control violence. Alert the State Guard."

Just then an explosion sounded from a few miles away and attention was jolted to that direction. Soon the western sky was lit up by a red and yellow blaze leaping upward and outward from the center of the city.

"My God," someone screamed, "it's the University of Amerika. The bankers are burning the university!"

"Anarchy!" shouted the chief of the Student's Bureau.

"Fascists!" shouted one of the marchers.

"We must have Law and Order!" shouted the People's Police.

No Joy in the Morning

She walked into the kitchen slowly, fumbling with the ties of her robe, still trying to slip one foot into her slipper. Unseeing, she got out the coffee and with annoyance ran the can into the electric can opener.

Why didn't I open this can last night, she asked herself—thirsty for a cup of coffee and impatient about having to fix it. With the coffee pot fixed and plugged in at last, she sat down dejectedly at the table and lit a cigarette.

A cry came from the back porch, and she unthinkingly opened it to let in a fat grey cat. She sat back down and puffed her cigarette, staring at the recently painted walls half-noticing how bright they were, but not so bright as to hide the cracked old plaster underneath.

Thud! The plastic bag of garbage she'd left by the sink fell over as the cat dug into it snooping for last night's remains of meat.

She jumped up with a strong desire to kick the cat, and screamed, "You, damn lousy cat!"

Frustrated and angry, she threw the cat out the back door, but not hard enough to hurt him. It was all she could do not to pound the walls as she ran her hand over her grey hair and stared at the gloomy life-less kitchen.

"Goddam lousy world," she almost screamed and then wanted to laugh, for she knew if she did scream there was no one near enough to hear, and even if they did, she would just be ignored.

She looked at the wooden shelves above the sink, the old sink that couldn't be changed when the rest of the kitchen was painted with the desire to try to modernize, brighten up, and bring

life to this old worn-out house off by itself. The shelves held can
after can of soups, vegetables, fruits, meats . . .

Again the impulse to scream rose in her. "Him and his
damned canned goods—his damn, damned canned goods!"
And the hurt, frustrated smile broke out. It's like having my
blood in a can—by God that's what he'll do when I die. Put my
blood up in cans—and this time she did cry.

She lay her head on the table and sobbed and sobbed until
some of the pain was gone. Then with a deep sigh, she leaned
back lighting another cigarette and thought, "Christ said Man
cannot live by bread alone—how true, how true."

And then she clutched the table with the old terror back in
her heart. She could see her husband with his cold, mocking eyes
standing in front of her, and his words came flashing to her
mind: "Try to live without bread."

The Artist

A friend of mine paints. Paints beautiful, but weird, abstract canvases which stir the emotions, and which no one comprehends. At a recent exhibition of her paintings, I noticed a new one that particularly attracted my attention. Like the others, it was an abstract pattern, but this one seemed to stand out more vividly than the others and was like a puzzle challenging the observer to decipher its meaning. Not being a student of art, I didn't know what to look for in a painting, but I stood off at various angles trying to analyze this sphinx-like canvas before me. It was titled "Autumn Leaves," and I tried in vain to find the leaves. What I did find were geometric designs framed in shades of brown and gray, with a large blob of what looked like scrambled eggs containing whole yolks ready to descend into the neat cubes and triangles. Or perhaps it was a sunburst, a complete galaxy of sunbursts, and the geometric patterns were the various elements of the revolving planets. But what does this have to do with autumn leaves?

My friend left a group of her admirers and came over to greet me. "You look puzzled," she stated, "don't you like it?"

We were old friends and understood each other. "Well . . ." I laughed, "it really intrigues me, but why is it called 'Autumn Leaves'? I don't see any leaves or anything resembling autumn."

She laughed in return and said, "These are Autumn Leaves as I see them." She then added, "One of these days remind me to tell you a story about this picture."

A few weeks later we were having dinner together and I asked her about the story.

"I was eight years old when I first tried to paint," she began. "I had been on a Sunday drive with my family and coming home in the bright fall afternoon the road we were on wove in and out along the Ohio River. I lay back against the seat of the car drowsily watching the tall maple trees all a blaze of reds and yellows staring at their reflections in the water. I was fascinated by this sight and for days could think of nothing else.

"With a dime store paint set and a roll of butcher paper, I tried to recreate my remembrance of the trees and their reflections in the water. But nothing I could do pleased me. My vain attempts looked like what they were, childish daubs of paint.

"Years later, as a teenager showing some talent for drawing, I tried again to put on paper my childish impression. But I still didn't like it. All I had been able to do was show trees, their leaves bright with color, their images reflected in the gray water. Something was missing.

"After five more years of working with art, when I was a student at the University, I finally realized what was missing in this picture I had attempted so often. I had just won a prize for my latest painting, again of the autumn leaves, and still I wasn't satisfied. The trees were there with all their color, the quiet muddy water of the Ohio was there, and the tall reflections of the trees rippling in the water were there, but that was it. They were only autumn leaves after all. A common sight.

"The image I'd been trying to create was a child's first awareness of beauty. The awakening of the artistic soul. And the stirring emotion of this scene had been in myself, not in the trees."

My friend leaned across the table towards me and continued in an excited but serious tone, "Do you see what I mean? A camera reproduces pictures of existing created life. But an artist—a real artist—takes the raw materials of life, such as ideas, thoughts, and emotions, and gives them form. Everyone's life experiences consist of emotions and perceptions, and you can't see, for instance, without using all your other senses at the same time and experiencing some particular emotion at some level. Each person sees differently for the experience of his senses and how his emotions and thoughts integrate these experiences is different."

She leaned back more relaxed now and went on, "So you see,

this is a painting of my total experience when I see or recall autumn leaves."

I understood what she had been telling me, and yet, the painting of "Autumn Leaves" flashed across my mind and I was still puzzled.

My friend saw the perplexed look on my face and laughed in her usual light and gay manner. "Never mind," she said. "those who say they understand my work don't really do so. With you, I can be honest. Right now I'm popular, but I realize this is probably just a novelty and will eventually end."

Later that night I lay in bed thinking of all she had told me and I wondered was the world yet ready for art such as hers? Or perhaps was she, in so much of her primitive simplicity, yet ready for this world? But we are still friends, and I follow her work and continue to be puzzled over the forms, while she continues to laugh at me and the rest of the world in her friendly way.

Hell's Playground

It was in Hell's Playground that I first fell in love. Wildly, completely, and painfully in love as a woman is capable of doing at only two times in her life. First, when she is still a young girl and becomes aware of the power of sex with all its mystery and wonder. She looks upon her beloved, her knees go weak, there is an emptiness in the pit of her stomach, and she realizes all her life has been a preparation for this moment. Then the pain enters when she knows she cannot fulfill her destiny, for reason enters and says do not touch. Family and society have taught her that this moment of beauty and truth is forbidden, and their hold on her is stronger than the primitive emotion she is experiencing. The second time in a woman's life when she is suscept-ible to this emotion arrives in mid-life. Sex is no stranger to her; she has lived with it for years. She has known moments of deep fulfillment, of excitement, and of boredom and disappointment. She has lain contentedly experiencing her womanhood, and she has learned to make love while mentally planning the next day's household chores. If anyone had asked her opinion of sex, which they never do, or if she had asked herself, which she never does, she would shrug and say, "I can take it or leave it." Then comes a time in mid-life when the primitive emotions awaken and whis-per you are about to lose that which you have never fully pos-sessed. And she is once again capable of wild, complete, and painful abandonment. Society no longer says forbidden, or if it does, she doesn't care. She is able to fulfill her desires, but pain-fully, for reason again enters and this time says you are middle-aged, the mother of grown children; you are making a fool of yourself and should retain your dignity. Then, also, with the wisdom of her years she knows this new love can't be permanent, and she lives in fear of the day she will lose it. Sex has many moods, many ways of expression, but neither dignity nor permanence have ever been one of them, and thus she suffers. And thus, wild, complete love is ever painful. But enough of women and their strange emotions. This story is about Hell's Playground as it existed long ago when "Stardust" was everyone's favorite song, and the world was at peace.

It was in the Fall of 1946, and Hell's Playground was an amusement park built on the edge of the sea, bordering a mile of a Southern Californian seaport town. The town was full of sailors, and the ones I came to know had just arrived in port from the Bikini bomb tests. The war had been over for a year, and these servicemen were the boys who had enlisted when the vets, the heroes of World War II, had won the war and returned to their wives and mothers, and many to children they had never seen.

I was sixteen in 1946, and the year since the war ended had seemed like an eternity, as it does when you are very young. But I remembered the war. It had started on a rainy Sunday while I was at the movies. We came outside the theater and heard newsboys shouting about the attack on Pearl Harbor. Three and a half years later, on a bright August day, the war ended. The news reached me at my summer job as sales clerk in a downtown department store where I'd lied about my age and gotten hired because low-paid help was hard to get. Everything closed for the day, and I fought my way to the bus station through a cheering crowd of servicemen wanting to hug and kiss me. I had been too young to understand the meaning of war that rainy Sunday in 1941, and I was too young to enjoy the celebrating crowd that unforgettable day in August, 1945. My role in the war had been going to movies, where I cheered the Marines and hissed and booed at the Japs. The war was never entirely real to me, for no one I loved or knew well was called to fight for our country. I knew there were men dying in the war, but I didn't know these men. In the same manner, I knew that when I was very young there had been hard times, a depression, and my grandparents had stood in bread lines, but I couldn't remember ever going without food or shelter. For years I erroneously believed these two events, the depression of the thirties and the world war of the forties, never touched my life. For how can you know depression when you are a child with no understanding of anything else? And how can you know war when you don't know adolescence without a war? And then it was 1946; these events were past and America was living in victory and prosperity, and I was unaware of this, for I had never been sixteen before. As a child, life meant my personal experiences. I didn't know I was living in history. History was a subject taught in school. It was the American Revolution, the Greeks and the Romans, and a lot of English kings. I didn't know that the world events I was living with would live forever in books and the minds of persons while I would die and be completely forgotten. Youth lives in a world of its own, a world of immortality where the past is dead, and the future has no meaning.

And so these youth in the navy went to Bikini and tested the bomb, never knowing they were ushering in the atomic age. Back in port, they enjoyed the pleasures of youth and of men in the service amid the enthusiastic spirit of the times, the spirit of victorious postwar America. None of these youth thought ahead or imagined the cold war and the space race to come. Some mentioned that maybe we'd have to fight Russia some day, mentioned it whimsically, for they had missed the war their older brothers had been in, and male youth still believed in the glory of war at that time. But none took the thought too seriously, for wasn't Russia our ally? Everyone remembered the pictures of Stalin and Roosevelt smiling and shaking hands during the many conferences of the Big Three. Besides we were the victors! We had saved the world from the powers of the Axis, we had ended the war, and we had the bomb! The bomb that was our insurance of supremacy in any future war.

The young sailors who descended upon California in 1946 were from all over America. Freckled faces from the farms of the Midwest, boys from upper middle class homes in the East, Blacks from the South experiencing integration for the first time, teenagers who didn't finish school and wouldn't return, and others whose college applications were waiting. With different backgrounds and personalities, at home they would have never met, but in the service together they became buddies, for they all had this in common: home was far away, and their remaining enlistment was for a long time. Some had girls at home, and maybe

they would wait, maybe not. Many of these boys were too young
to vote, but too old to ever be a child again. They were away from
home for the first time, and they were men now; men like their
big brothers who had won the war. All the gaudy, sensational life
of Southern California welcomed them. Service men were still
heroes at this time and there were always many places to go
where they didn't ask for I.D.'s. These youth proved their new
manhood by frequenting the bars and the brothels, by outdrink-
ing and outboasting each other.

Hell's Playground was not the real name of this California
amusement park. It had a typical name, like Coney Island, although that wasn't it. I've long ago forgotten its actual name, and
the one time I returned after many years away, I didn't care to
notice what this park was called. To me, it was always Hell's
Playground. Bennie had suggested the name one night when we
sat on a bench in this park and I had poured out my dreams to
him. At that time I wanted two things in life—Johnny, the sailor
I had fallen in love with, and to finish school and write novels.
Laughingly, I told Bennie my first novel would be about this
amusement park. We talked about it and searched for a name.

"Hell's Playground," Bennie said, and the name stuck.

Dear old Bennie. He was one of Johnny's best friends and
always seemed to be around when Johnny wasn't. Like that Friday night when things were going wrong. Johnny had twenty-
four hour liberty and had phoned me to meet him at the bus stop
across the street from the park. Like a child anticipating Christmas, I had sat in the bus with my eyes closed knowing that when I
opened them Johnny would be with me.

The bus stopped and people began getting off. I opened my
eyes and searched through the window for a tall, dark, curly-
haired sailor with laughing, reckless eyes and a cleft in his chin.
My eyes met Bennie's and he waved. With growing apprehen-
sion, I got off the bus and kept searching, but no Johnny.

"Johnny couldn't make it, kid. He got duty," Bennie stated
and then continued, "He told me I should tell you."

A deep disappointment swept over me and I felt like all the
city lights had dimmed and I was alone, the only one in the world
alone, as I was acutely aware of sailors and their girls walking by
arm in arm.

"Damn," I muttered, "I haven't seen him for a week."

Bennie stood there talking, but I didn't hear what he said. The blood began rushing from the emptiness in my stomach, and I blurted out, "I don't believe it! I don't believe it, Bennie. He had duty all week." I stared into the thick glasses Bennie wore, trying to find his eyes behind the lenses. "He's out on a binge, isn't he? Tell me the truth!"

Bennie averted my eyes, but reached down quickly and took my hand. "C'mon kid, I'll buy you a cup of coffee."

He steered me around the corner towards a coffee shop, but I stopped at the door, angrier than ever now.

"I don't want coffee," I shouted at him, "I want a drink. I want to get drunk. I want to know what it's like."

"Come on," Bennie insisted firmly, pulling me towards the coffee shop door.

"No!" I jerked away from him and started across the street not noticing the light was red. A horn blared and brakes squealed.

Bennie was at my side squeezing my arm until it hurt. "You damn crazy kid," he said, angry now, "You stubborn moron! All right. I'll buy you a drink."

I blinked back the tears that were forcing themselves to my eyes and let Bennie lead me across the street.

We walked down the concrete steps leading to Hell's Playground and approached the gaudy lights, signs, and music drifting from all directions. I had my mind on one place, The House of Blue Lights. It was a small club with its back turned to the beauty of the Pacific Ocean, the never-ending jazz music blaring above the rhythmic crash of the breakers. With standing room only, the sailors lined up nightly to hear the Black singer, Molly, go into her rendition of the song the club was named after. Johnny would never take me here.

"Here," I said, jerking away from Bennie's still firm grip on my arm. "I want to go here."

"They'll ask your age here," he stated.

"Nobody ever asks my age," I answered defiantly.

"O.K., O.K. But if we get kicked out, don't say I didn't tell ya' so."

We were lucky and got a small table in a dark corner. We had to nudge our way into the chairs, the tables were so close together. Bennie bumped the table next to us and the couple sitting

there grabbed their drinks and stared up at him. The man was a
heavy set Marine, and he looked at Bennie with hostility.

"Sorry, Buddie," Bennie said in what I thought was a conde-
scending tone.

The Marine grunted, however, and turned his eyes back to
the blonde he was with.

A scantily clad cocktail waitress appeared at our table. "What
will you have?" she asked.

"Rum and coke," I blurted as she looked at Bennie.

"Two rums and cokes," Bennie carried through.

She looked over at me and I stared into her eyes, daring her
to ask my age. She didn't. She shrugged and walked towards the
bar. God, how awful she looks with all that make-up, I thought.
She must be at least thirty-five years old. Why do women always
try to hide their age when all the time they just emphasize it? I
imagined myself thirty-five years old with puffy eyes outlined in
green, thick beigy make-up that cracked if I smiled too hard, big
red patches for cheeks, and a scarlet gash for a mouth. I shud-
dered.

The drinks arrived and I reached out eagerly for the tall
glass. I removed the cherry and popped it into my mouth savor-
ing the crunchy feel of bursting the outer skin, then washed it
down with the dark liquid. It was sweet, too sweet, and I wished I
had ordered something else, but I took another big drink and
this time it tasted better.

Bennie said something but I couldn't hear him above the
noise of the music and the people.

"What?" I leaned towards him.

"Don't gulp the stuff," he said, "drink it slow. It's better for
you."

I'll darn well do what I please, I wanted to answer, but instead
just glared at him. He turned his attention to the five piece band
blowing away in the back of the room on a raised platform above
a small crowded dance floor. I took another drink, and my anger
began to subside. I felt guilty about glaring at Bennie. After all,
he had brought me here. He was really a nice guy, but he wasn't
Johnny. Johnny! Oh damn him, damn him! Where is he? I wanted to cry again, so I took another drink. I sipped it this time, slow
but continuously, and looked at Bennie. He wouldn't be bad
looking without those glasses; of course he couldn't compare to
Johnny, beautiful, beautiful Johnny, but he was a nice guy. He

was good to me. Why wasn't Johnny good to me? Why didn't I
fall in love with a guy like Bennie? But he was a Jew. He wouldn't
ever marry me. Jews won't marry gentile girls. Someone had
once told me this but I couldn't remember who. Besides, I was
going to marry Johnny. He had said so. In sixteen months when
he got out of the navy, and I got out of school. Married. Johnny
and I. I tipped my glass to my lips but it was empty.

Another replaced it. My, this was an efficient place. Real E-
fficient! I admired efficiency. I wished I was efficient. If I was I'd
know how to hold on to Johnny. But he loved me. I knew he did.

"That whore?"

"Hell, why not?"

They were getting louder at the table on the other side of us
and I was jolted out of my reverie. There were four of them. Two
young ones and two older ones with stripes on their sleeves.
Bos'ns, I thought, navy regulars I'd heard Johnny call them. I
listened to them.

"Burinski got the clap from her," one of the young ones
stated. He looked a little like Johnny in his cocky white hat and
tight fitting navy blues.

One of the older men laughed at this. It was a deep, toothless
laugh, and I stared at him fascinated. "Shit!" he said, "you green
kids make me laugh. You're not a man 'til you've had at least one
dose. It's no wors'n a bad cold."

Johnny. A bad cold. Johnny has a bad cold; that's why he isn't
here. No. Not a cold. The clap. Johnny has the clap. I'll get it.
But I haven't slept with him. You don't have to. Just kissing. Is
that true? I don't know. Who can I ask? Bennie? Yes, I'll ask
Bennie. He knows everything.

"Bennie," I leaned towards him.

"Yeah?"

"I want to go home."

And Bennie took me home. He always did when I needed
someone. We walked the eight blocks from the bus stop to my
house, slowly and talking all the way.

"Bennie, why did Johnny stand me up?"

"He's just wild," Bennie said. "He'll get it out of his system."

"But does he really love me?"

"How in the hell should I know?"

"Well you don't have to get mad."

"I'm not mad," he answered softly. "You're such a crazy kid.

You're both crazy kids. You deserve each other. You'll go back to that town in Kansas, or wherever the hell it is, and live in a rose-covered cottage full of fat-cheeked kids."

"Do you really think so?" I asked eagerly. "But his mother keeps writing not to get engaged because nice girls don't live in California."

"You deserve it, and the mother-in-law too," Bennie said, "the way you act."

"What do you mean by that?" I asked. Bennie was always confusing me.

"Don't mind me," he answered, "I just don't buy the American dream, that's all. If you had grown up where I did, you might know what I mean."

"In New York you mean?"

"Yeah. On the rough side. You should see the American dream there."

"Bennie," I asked curiously, "Johnny once said you were a Communist. Is that true?"

He laughed and asked, "Do you know what a Communist is?"

"Well sure," I answered a little indignantly, "it's someone working for Russia."

"That's what I thought you'd say."

"Well—what is it then?"

"Skip it. Keep your American dream."

"You're a funny guy. I've never known anyone like you."

We walked on in silence and my mind returned to Johnny. "Bennie," I blurted, "do you think I should sleep with Johnny?"

"Why in the hell do you ask me?" he answered angrily.

"Who can I ask? My mother?" I was angry now too, but added, "I thought you were my friend."

Bennie was quiet. Then he said softly, "He's probably sterile anyway. I've read a bit, and thought a lot about it, and all of us who were at Bikini stand a good chance of being sterile."

"That's some consolation."

"Well, it's something to think about if you really plan to marry him and want to have kids."

"I'm not worried about having kids; it's not having kids I'm worried about."

"Well," Bennie said, "sleep with him and take a chance."

"Oh, sure," I said glumly.

"What have you got to lose?"

"Not much! Just—my parents would kick me out, Johnny might sail away and never marry me, and I wouldn't get to finish school. Not much."

"Then remain a virgin."

"And lose Johnny?"

"That's life, kid."

"Thanks a lot for the advice."

"You asked for it."

That was Bennie. With me he was always a kind and some-what serious person. He replaced the big brother I always wished I had. Johnny insisted that Bennie really enjoyed the wild life of the navy. I told Johnny about him worrying about the effects of radioactivity and the possibility that all the men who were at Bikini might be sterile. Johnny laughed hard and said, "Oh he worries, alright. Worries about how many women he can con-vince he's sterile."

"But Johnny," I insisted, "I've never ever seen him with a woman."

"He keeps them in private," Johnny answered.

"What do you mean?" I asked curiously.

"Don't worry your pretty little head over things that don't concern you," he answered, and stopped my questions, as he always did, with a kiss.

And that was Johnny. Wild and reckless, but gentle and lov-ing. Not showing up when I had waited so long to see him, then phoning two days later to ask if I'd missed him. Then before I could get angry, he'd say something about my not wanting to see him any more, and somehow I always ended up feeling sorry for him, and loving him all the more.

We would meet again at the bus stop across from Hell's Play-ground, and Johnny would eagerly grab my hand and smile in that beautiful, teasing way that only he had and say, "C'mon baby, this is *our* night." We would go once again to Hell's Play-ground and mingle with the crowd. Everything young sailors and their girls could possibly want was there. A dance hall, ice cream and hot dog stands, games of chance and rides of thrill, the roller coaster winding over the sea, the loop-de-loop, ferris wheel and tunnel of love, the shouts: "Guess your age, weight, or home state," "C'mon sailor, win a doll for the lady," "How about a picture to send home?" From all sides they came, the painted women in tight sweaters or low-necked blouses, the gypsy who knew all, the old men with sly smiles.

When the bars closed at two a.m., the coffee shops took over. By four a.m. the streets were quiet. Only an old man who picked up papers and trash was seen in Hell's Playground. Sailors who had money and a pass stayed at a low-priced hotel across the street. Those who had a pass and no money went to the all-night movies. If they had a girl, they sat in the back row sleeping with their arms around each other.

At eight a.m. Sunday morning, Hell's Playground took on its respectable air. The pier was crowded with men, women and children, all in blue jeans, baiting their hooks and staring into the blue surf of the Pacific. There was no sign saying Fishermen Only, but anyone going near felt this unspoken rule in the faces of the people. In a small park a group of old men sat at picnic tables playing cards. In the afternoon a band played on a stage in the park. The senior citizens unpacked picnic lunches and listened to the music of Strauss and Sousa.

It was on a Sunday like this that I met Johnny. I had been to Hell's Playground one time since my arrival in Southern California to live with my father and his new wife. They had picked me up at the Greyhound depot and then brought me here to see the town, as they said. I was too tired to enjoy anything, but a desire to see more stayed in my mind. The many weekends I was alone I thought of returning, but the natural shyness of a girl barely sixteen prevented me until one Sunday overcome with boredom and restlessness, I took the bus downtown. Timidly, I approached the entrance to Hell's Playground, trying to appear inconspicuous, a lone girl amid this crowd of roving sailors. I was sitting on a bench in front of the roller coaster listening to Hoagy Carmichael sing, "Ole Buttermilk Sky," when a tall, handsome sailor walked up and asked me the time. His boyish grin looked harmless, and before I knew what happened we were being carried at breath-taking speed over the dips and curves of the roller coaster, his arm around me, and his hand squeezing mine.

Thus began the days of my first love. I was wildly, completely, and painfully in love with a twenty-year-old sailor from a small town in the Midwest. I lived for the nights Johnny had liberty and we would go to Hell's Playground. On the dark, empty pier, our backs to the amusement park, the jazz music from the House of Blue Lights drifting out to us, and only the endless expanse of

sea and sky in front of us, we'd plan our future and swear that
our love would last forever.

When I didn't see Johnny, the days were long and empty. In
spite of my strong desire to finish school, I found my studies and
my classmates boring, only crammed for necessary exams, and
made almost no friends. Without realizing it, my life with Johnny and his shipmate-buddies had passed me into an adult world
where I'd never again be the timid school girl who approached
Hell's Playground that lonely Sunday. Also, I soon learned there
was really no place for me in the life of my father and his wife,
although they both took a parental stand against my relationship
with Johnny. Their disapproval combined with his mother's disapproval caused Johnny to write to me saying we shouldn't see
each other anymore. I was devastated and fought my parents
then. I won their permission to go with Johnny, but the seeds of
insecurity had been planted and to nurture the seeds was the
continual expectation of his orders to sail.

Eventually, as happens to all men of the sea, my sailor left
port. Johnny wrote every day at first, and I kept his letters in a
purple velvet case made for this alone. He swore to return and be
with me when I graduated from school and after that I'd become
his wife. As the weeks turned into months, the letters became less
and less. When he was discharged in San Francisco a year later,
he went straight home to the Midwest and I never saw him again.
I graduated from school alone and left Southern California.
Eventually I married, and for years I kept a purple velvet case
filled with letters in a bottom dresser drawer.

Sixteen years later I returned to Hell's Playground. It looked
about the same as I had remembered. A few new attractions had
been added, but all the old ones remained. It was less crowded
than in 1946, but still full of sailors. I walked out on the pier and
gazed at the sea. I sat on the same bench by the roller coaster
where I had met Johnny, and I paused by the door of the House
of Blue Lights which had a different name now and a new Black
singer singing a different blues song. Hell's Playground was still
the same, I thought, but the magic was gone. I was no longer
sixteen and in love. I was no longer sixteen where the future is a
distant dream and history exists only in books. The young servicemen who now haunted Hell's Playground were the war babies from the past. All they knew of war were the tales told by

their dads, and all they knew of peace was the atomic age. Their
time in history was the cold war, the space race, and the dawning
social consciousness of America. These sailors sought the thrills
of all young servicemen away from home for the first time, but
their search was not the celebration of '46 that I had shared. It
was the increasing feelings of urgency and guilt of 1962. Few
foresaw the difficulties that would arise from our, at that time,
minor commitment in the Far East, or the internal struggles
ahead in the sixties. The job of these servicemen was not to fight
a war, for, except for a few scattered servicemen fighting in far-
off places, conventional warfare was gone; nor was their job to
test bombs, for the major powers in the world had enough weapons with enough megatons to destroy the world. Their job was
only to stand by in case they were needed—needed for what,
they weren't sure. There had been talk of a possible invasion of
Cuba, but Khrushchev had backed down under Kennedy's ad-
monitions during the Cuban blockade, while the rest of America
waited in fear of nuclear warfare.

I watched the sailors and girls walking by doing the same
things my sailor and I had done in our day. As we had reflected
the spirit of 1946 without knowing it, I saw the spirit of 1962 in
these young faces. This was a serious world they had inherited.
This was America, no longer the victor, no longer the savior of
the world, no longer the supreme power. The Soviet Union had
A bombs and H bombs now; the Soviet Union had put up the
first satellite, and the Soviet Union had the first man in orbit.
The race to be first on the moon was in full progress, and we
were behind in this race, as we were behind in the cold war. We
had won the war and saved the world for democracy, but we had
lost our victory. In shame, the world now remembered Hiroshi-
ma and viewed with different eyes the March of Bataan and the
men who fell on Corregidor and Guadalcanal. During the Nur-
emburg trials, there were those who pointed their finger at
America saying how dare we speak of Nazi atrocities after what
we had done. The pride and prestige of 1946 had turned to
defeat by 1962. The bomb we gave birth to cast a shadow over
the world; the war we had won turned into a cold war of nerves
and fear, and our prosperity, once viewed as great, had given rise
to guilt. In 1946 the world had been larger. The feeling that we
had done our job well and could go home and forget the rest of
the world had disappeared. With jets, rockets, and push button

weapons, the world had become smaller and peace had vanished, perhaps forever. But enough of history, all this will live on in books long after young sailors and their girls are completely forgotten.

I returned to the bench by the roller coaster and listened to a rock 'n roll tune from a nearby juke box while my mind went back nostalgically to the music of Hoagy Carmichael and the immortal "Stardust." A sailor and his girl walked by, their arms around each other, and the thought came to me—how cheap they look. I examined the girl, closely noticing how her clothes and hair showed a lack of taste, and another thought came to my mind—as mine had done those many years ago, and for a moment I felt shame for what I had been. Then a line of poetry floated to me—If thou regrettest thy youth, why live? But I didn't regret my youth. I had loved, and I had known only beauty—the beauty of happiness and the beauty of sorrow. But now the magic was gone. I looked around and realized that Hell's Playground was just a rather shabby amusement park full of ordinary people.

I watched another couple, a tall sailor and a young bleached blonde, walking towards the pier. Were they in love, I wondered. How should I know? But their look of self-satisfaction irritated me. Again poetry flashed to my mind, and I wondered why this always happens when I think about love. I dwelt on the words and thought perhaps the poet was right when he said—In her first passion woman loves her lover, in all the others, all she loves is love.

With this thought I rose from the bench, turned my back on this playground, and left. Left Hell's Playground to the next generation of sailors and girls. Maybe someday one of them would find a love that would last forever, and maybe someday the world would find a peace that also would last forever.

Precious

This is the story of my cat. She and I have been alone for a long time now. I worry about her because I know how fragile she is and that she could never survive in the streets if anything happens to me. This is why her story must be written.

She and I have become very attached to each other. Many times I only go home because I know she is lonely. We have been living in a one room apartment and she is sad that I am so unhappy, but she wants to be with me in spite of our circumstances. She tries to comfort me and many times when I feel I can't make it any longer, I hold her tightly in my arms with my tears falling into her fur, and I talk to her and tell her, it's O.K., it's O.K., we'll make it, and then when my feelings of desperation subside, she licks my face with her tongue until I'm relaxed again.

Although she has been very lonely since my children left us, sometimes she only sees me when I am asleep, and sometimes I have left her for a few days, she handles it well now—not like before.

She is an easy cat to care for. She eats only Little Friskies and has a small appetite. She makes no messes and gives much loyalty and affection in return for her needs. She loves to stretch in the sunshine, like all cats, and to climb to high places, and she quietly sees everything that is going on. She likes people and is especially happy when someone comes to visit. She is not timid, but also not aggressive. She will climb into people's laps without invitation, but if they push her away she leaves without feeling slighted.

She gets along with other cats also. When my children lived with us, we always had other cats. Sometimes, she gets very playful with other cats and it is fun to watch her because she is never playful alone. She never bothers other cats and is not greedy over food. She will hold back and wait patiently for her turn. If the other cats bother her when she needs food, or rest, or to be alone, she will fight them off in such a way that they are shocked and respect her in a new way and don't try it again. Then they are friends once more.

Last summer, I had the opportunity to get an all-black male kitten, and I realized that I had always wanted a black cat and I was very happy. I was happy because I wanted him for myself, but also I felt happy because my cat would now have company while I was gone. I think she fell in love with this kitten at first sight. She would sit back and watch his playful antics and her eyes sparkled with warmth and pleasure. She even joined him in his games and I was happy watching the two of them. She seemed at times to be saying, "Who is this strange new animal whose ways I am so unfamiliar with, but how delightful he is to be with, and what a joy not to be alone now."

I had been told the kitten was house trained, but I soon found out it wasn't true. I would come home at night and find the kitten's excrements in all the corners of my room. I would scrub the floor and spray it with Lysol—the smell was especially strong due to the hot weather—and I was hopeful and had good advice on training the kitten. It didn't work. He had a strong aversion to the cat box and all my efforts failed.

Then there was another problem. I would fall asleep at night and awaken to find the kitten entangled in my hair. All efforts to stop this also failed. In desperation, I had to shut the cat in the bathroom so I could sleep. He cried all night and both my cat and I felt sad about this.

One very hot Friday, I came home to my smelly apartment and I knew the kitten had to go. I drank a whole bottle of Strawberry Hill wine, and I cried, and then I took him back to the girlfriend who gave him to me. She was angry because her advice on how to train him had not worked, and she didn't want to talk to me. I felt very sad also thinking about my children and that if they had been with me perhaps the kitten could have been trained.

It took weeks to clean the carpet and get the smell out of the apartment. Cat and I have been alone ever since then. We have had some very hard times, and I have been tempted to seek a good home for her, but I feel she would rather be unhappy with me than well-cared-for elsewhere.

Fortunately, her appetite is very small, so I have always been able to feed her. When my children lived with us, we received food stamps from the welfare department, but we were told that animals are a luxury and cat food can't be bought with food stamps. When I was in court my ex-husband claimed $100 a month for pet food, and the judge considered it a legitimate need, but then he had bought a goat, and maybe that's not considered a luxury. When I had difficulty feeding three children and myself on $96 a month, I was told I needed help to learn more about nutrition and how to handle a budget, and I attended a seminar where I heard that it really is a shame that so many people do not know how to care for themselves, and we need more trained experts to teach nutrition to welfare recipients.

I think I realized about this time that almost all of my life someone or other had been telling me how to adjust. I became angry then, and decided it was time for the world to make a few adjustments to my needs. I asked a lawyer and a social worker if they could raise three children on $210 a month, and they told me, of course they could, and I was a grown woman, and had to adjust. Also, the court was concerned about the financial pressures on my ex-husband, and didn't know that he only moved off the ranch and into an apartment to show more expenses, and that he'd move back when the divorce was settled. The court was also concerned about his obligations to his parents, and the court did know, but like the pet food considered it a legitimate expense, that he had borrowed so much money from his parents to drag the divorce over almost two years and fight for custody of the children. Like all good things, the divorce was settled eventually, and I received custody of our children, and he received custody of our money and obligation to his parents. The children and I then became dependent on the State for aid. Due to my failure to adjust, the children are gone now and only cat and I hold out still hoping for that better life we dreamed about when we ran away from my ex-husband and his parents.

I found cat when I was still married. I was living with my husband in a very old and very cold house which sat on his parents' prune ranch. Cat came from across the creek where there was a new housing development of very special executive homes. The ranch we lived on was also now surrounded by very special executive homes with swimming pools and stables, but my husband's parents held on to their land in spite of lucrative offers, and complained loudly about the cost of taxes which came to more than the profit of the prunes. One day, I became angry, maybe because I didn't sincerely feel sorry for them, and I said if they wanted to raise prunes they needed to move to a farming area which this no longer was, or they could retire, as they claimed to have around a half million saved. They told me I was crazy. My ex-husband tried to prove this in court. That was why I nearly lost my children and why I received no adequate financial assistance. A crazy woman must learn to adjust. I also just happened to be going to college and the judge was very firm about the fact that this was definitely not good for my mental health. It was only much later that I came to fully recognize the philosophy—if you help someone, they will never learn how to do it for themselves. Social workers are strong adherents of this policy that you hurt someone by helping them. Only recently do I see the full validity of this, and I no longer fight the world. For example—if someone had helped me fix my so-very-old and so-very-broken-down automobile that first year of adjustment, I would have never learned how to do it myself; but then I never learned how to do it anyway, but that is another story about my lack of mechanical ability.

I had to withdraw from a college class one time because, as the university counselor said, I was trying to be an automobile mechanic, a lawyer, a father, a mother, and a student, too. I was also working part-time and I lied to the welfare department so they wouldn't take it away from me, and I became very frightened. I believed they could put me in jail for cheating, and, of course, they could. The world is outraged at people who cheat on welfare because *their* tax money is paying for *your* children's food. No one ever blames the father for not paying more, and the investigators who pried into our lives, and even asked the children who they wanted to live with, never investigated the father's financial pressures to see if he paid back his obligations to his parents, who of course didn't need it anyway as they had bank books sitting in coffee cans in the kitchen showing their half a million dollars; and also they never spent money, preferring to live with a wood burning stove and outdoor toilet, and raise prunes they lost money on. But that's another story. I recently heard two women in a supermarket talking and they agreed they would like to go on food stamps so they could eat butter and steak and drink wine. I wanted to tell them you can't buy wine, as well as cat food, on food stamps. But then I realized that if you drink wine when you're on welfare, only God can save you. Even my children became outraged as my wine drinking increased, and I got angry one day and told them to *never* criticize anything I do unless they have gone through what I have. They went to live with their father then, where they have all the money they want, no worries, and no work. Whenever a problem arises he still blames me for not adjusting, and now my children see it his way.

Only cat knows why I come home and drink wine. I once had a friend who knew, but as times got harder and I still wouldn't adjust, he, too, got angry at my willfullness and is no longer my friend. I know some very respectable people who drink lots of hard liquor even but then it's O.K. because they always pay their bills on time. It really isn't always easy to drink a bottle of Red Mountain when you owe two months' rent.

But back now to the day I met cat. My neighbors found her wandering down by the creek and she was very hungry and very frightened. Gradually, she began to eat with their cats. She was a beautiful Siamese, tiny and fragile for a full grown cat. I fell in love with her at first sight and took her home. I watched the ads but no one reported her missing. Thus she became mine. At that time everything that was mine also belonged to the whole family. I see now that my only real personal belongings were my books, and they were always half hid.

Our family had another cat at this time. He was large, fat, grey, ugly, named Tom, and my husband and children liked him. I tolerated him. After dinner everyone retired to the T.V. set while I cleaned the kitchen. Tom developed a habit of biting my leg to let me know he wanted the table scraps. Sometimes I threw him outside, sometimes I glared at him, but eventually I always fed him. Perhaps it was because I never knew what to do with the garbage. I tried once to get weekly garbage service, but this made my husband angry because it's not necessary when you live on a ranch. We threw all the garbage out by the orchard, and every six months my husband and his father bagged it in gunny sacks and carried it up a hill where they dug holes and buried it. My pleas for garbage service were seen only as another symptom of

my poor mental condition and refusal to adjust. My dislike of
old Tom was further proof. I think I always wanted to kick him,
but I had been taught to suppress all inherent desires to harm
animals. When I took basic psych. at college, I began to re-
evaluate my relationship with old Tom. I decided then to put
into practice what I had learned and to retrain this mean old cat
to be good to me if he wanted food. Like my failure to adjust,
which I have now accepted, my failure at using psychology on
animals I have also accepted. Old Tom was definitely smarter
than I. He was wise to my tricks and knew I still wanted to kick
him.

I named my Siamese cat Precious because she was very precious to me. I have since read that the Egyptians believed Siamese cats to be sacred. I felt compassion for this stray who was
so insecure that she ate large amounts of wool or anything resembling wool. The children's socks or sweaters were continually
attacked; she even ate at my husband's undershirts, and when
she was desperate she'd make big holes in blankets that were on
the beds. My husband and children did not like this about her
and were not very understanding of her problem. I think now
that maybe they were angry because she never ate any of my
clothing. Of course my clothes were never lying on the floor
waiting for someone to pick them up, but that's only an excuse
for the cat's failure to adjust.

One day before I gave in to my increasing hostility towards
mean old Tom, I took my three daughters—my son had run
away almost a year before, and I had wished him well and said I'd
like to go with him—and I ran away. A couple of weeks later,
some friends helped me sneak back one afternoon with a trailer,
and we took a little furniture, all my books, the girls' toys, and
Precious. After that the gate to the ranch was locked.

Precious was very frightened in the new environment and ate
holes in everything. Only gradually did she realize mean old
Tom was gone, and there was a balcony with sunshine, and she
relaxed more and more. The two bedroom apartment was always filled with neighborhood kids and more stray cats and
noise. However, Precious soon learned to adjust to each strange
new cat, and the three or four times that babies were born in the
bedroom closet on top of my daughters' clothing. It took the
support of a good friend each time to dispose of the baby kittens
as best we could. I tried explaining to my daughters that we

couldn't have eight or ten cats where in writing no pets were allowed. My daughters were very angry at me, however, and this action of mine was another proof of my lack of ability to adjust.

That first year when spring vacation came and the sun was glorious, I got angry again and insisted: we now lived in a two bedroom upstairs apartment, and my three girls had no room or need for twenty-four stuffed animals, ten Barbie dolls, sixteen games they never played, and eight boxes of outgrown clothing used only for cat-birth, or cat food when Precious was upset. I began spring cleaning, and everything we didn't use or need was going to go. Eventually, I gave in to the girls' pleas and agreed to take their belongings to their father. As he wasn't home, I deposited all their things over the fence of the garden apartment he lived in until the divorce was settled. This action was not only proof of my failure to adjust, it was strong evidence of the mental problems my ex-husband was convincing others that I suffered from.

About six weeks after this we returned to court to hear the findings of the probation department regarding my fitness as a mother, and the decision of the court regarding our welfare. Over a year had passed since I had run away, and the court decided that my mental problems were such that I needed to stay home and take better care of my children, to stop attending the university, to get a job commensurate with my present level of education, and to accept my husband's obligation to his parents and the hardships the divorce had caused him. Also, the court decided, it was not right for me to deprive the father of his children, so he was given joint custody which I was told meant he had one-half say on where the children went to college and everyday important decisions like that. I thank God the custody of the cats never came up, so there *is* mercy in this world of pure justice. He kept Tom and I kept Precious. I realize now that she is the only thing I have ever had that no one has threatened to take away from me.

My cat and I were apart for one month when I was ill. The pressures of the divorce and investigation of my fitness as a mother had been too much for me. I had asked for $350 a month for five years to care for the four of us while I finished an education. I walked out of the courtroom with $210 a month and a broken-down car. My husband had possession of the Mercedes, the sailboat, and everything else left on the ranch. I thought and thought over my situation: As a very young girl I had worked in the fields, then advanced to waitress, carhop and salesclerk. For twenty years I'd been a housewife and mother, and the last few a student. I was now entering my junior year at the university and had been accepted into the honors program. In a few more years I planned to graduate with a teaching credential and teach English in high school. Even with school loans, if I ever became eligible, I couldn't make it on $210 a month. The car wasn't running and the rent was overdue. The next day I called my social worker and asked if we couldn't have $12 worth of food stamps, because I didn't have $36 to pay for the $48 worth of coupons we received. We couldn't. Five more cats were born in the closet and my ex-husband was on the phone inviting the girls to a movie at cinerama. I was holding a three-day notice on the apartment when I began beating the walls.

My doctor put me in a hospital for crazy people. It was called a therapeutic community, but everyone knew what it was. It was the nicest place I've ever lived. The doors were always open, and I could come and go as I desired. There was no place I wanted to go. The hospital living room was a large sunlit room with blue sofas and easy chairs always filled with other patients, visitors, or staff members. I had three good meals a day served in the dining room where we sat at tables of four, and there was a refrigerator always filled with milk, juice, or soft drinks. I even had a room all to myself. Everyone was expected to take turns cleaning, and I enjoyed the living room with the stereo on and people around, but I avoided the kitchen. Many times I still don't know what to do with garbage, and one day I started crying when I remembered a time when I got angry at my ex-husband for yelling at the children to eat their dinner, and they were crying while he went on and on about the starving Korean children, so I put all the uneaten food in a box and told him to mail it to Korea. I think he never did like me after that, and he should have married a Korean woman with ten starving children and remained a marine sergeant, but anyway no one bites my leg anymore.

At the hospital I was able to play volleyball, ping-pong, card games, and even laugh and cry whenever I felt like it. How nice it was to take up where I had left off as a teenager! No one told me I was crazy when I said I wanted to play ping-pong. They might say they were tired and would join me later, or they felt too shitty, or something, but no one saw my desires as a sign of deviant behavior. Even the trained staff, and some were not too friendly, liked to see me having fun and even understood why I cried. I have heard that judges are opposed to women having therapy, and do use this against them. I won't even try to understand this. Deep in my heart I know I am glad I never adjusted to my husband's demands. I thank God every day that I was not a Korean woman with ten starving children, that I subversively read books from age six on, and that the custody of my cat never came up.

Precious has a hernia or something and when I was married and had money I asked a vet about it and he said it really should be taken care of but she wasn't in pain or anything. It bothers other people, but to me it doesn't mar her beauty. She used to have two saber teeth that people always commented on. Just last year they fell out. I wish I knew how old she is, and I guess someone who understands cats could give me an estimate, but I can't afford any more worries, and we live one day at a time doing the best we can, and if I ever go home and she is dead or something, I don't know what will happen to me. When my daughter tried to kill herself last year, people quit visiting me. She was living with her father and when I found out what happened I called the hospital and was crying and demanding information. I even got very angry at the doctor and told him I was an upset mother when he accused me of being on drugs and therefore not understanding clearly every word he said. I later learned that my ex-husband had explained to him that mental problems ran in the mother's side of the family, and also the mother was a college student, and—oh! I had forgotten that— the court had also assumed that women crazy enough to run away so they can go to college are also taking drugs, although the judge did stop my ex-husband's expensive attorney when he accused me of taking drugs and visiting men between classes, on the grounds of "hearsay' and said it would have to be investigated. This was when the Adult Probation Department took over our lives. Of course, the divorce I wanted was also postponed, and new laws came into effect the following year which influenced the settlement. My husband was also freed of obligations during the year of investigation, and the children and I were placed on welfare. I never took drugs, but I did go to court in tennis shoes and long hair. Maybe I was a late blooming flower child after all.

My son took drugs. After he ran away from home he wrote me a long letter about how he began to drop acid and how happy he was. He was living on the beach in Hawaii. He came home on my birthday to surprise me. At two a.m. there he was at the door just off the plane. We sat in the kitchen and drank hot chocolate and I forgot he was taking drugs all that night. It was shortly after that that I ran away and my son was very happy I'd made the break and he wanted me to take drugs so I'd be even happier. I refused, and he was angry and said I didn't want to help myself. Later he joined a religious group and gave up drugs and the world, including his family. He wanted me to join and give up the world also. This time I was angry at him and insisted, "You do your thing, let me do mine, and let's accept each other." I have not seen or heard from him since.

I keep forgetting I have a son. I have forgotten the days before I ran away. Forced to remember, I see my son as seventeen years old in his last year of school. He was an A student, track star, and bus boy. I see him in his room at home, the door always shut against three younger sisters, me sitting on his bed throwing darts, going to the restaurant where he worked for two years and the manager beaming that he was the best worker he ever had and sending me free drinks, dropping him off two blocks away so no one would know his mother was driving him when he was jumping with Stanford athletes, lying on the floor playing monopoly or yahtze telling his friends, "my mom's O.K.," my husband's continual anger and his words, "here comes the rah rah kid," saving dinner when we were all together to cut him down until he'd cry and go to his room, my husband going to the banquet and smilingly accepting praise for being the father of the "Outstanding Athlete of the Year," and also being the only father who had never met the coach or been to a game, refusing to sign for a driver's license after he passed the test with 96% when I failed mine after fifteen years of driving experience, my son spraining his ankle at a practice meet where he set a record and was one week away from the State finals, two years of savings from his restaurant job spent on a VW that broke down a month later and my ex-husband had to tow home and spent weeks bitterly working on until no one cared if it were fixed or not, and everything ending the night of high school graduation when the Seniors went to an all night chaperoned party and when my son came home his father was waiting and told him to leave. He slept in the park for a week and I begged my husband to bring him home. He was relentless. My son had planned to major in P.E. and History at college. His trophies still sit in my trunk, and I haven't a doubt that he would have made the Olympics. He was everything a mother could want in a son, but like me, he was too sensitive, and didn't know how to fight back.

This is supposed to be the story of my cat. It's funny how things don't turn out the way they are supposed to. Her name is still Precious and right now she is in my very dirty and lonely apartment waiting for me to come home. She has food and water and the sunshine that filters through the window and that is all she asks for anymore.

A few important details about Precious must be included before I finish. We have made three more moves since the first one when I ran away. She now adjusts to a new home in one day. She has also been completely cured of eating clothing. She still doesn't go outside very much, and, when she does, she wants the door open so she can get in and not become upset. Traveling in a car disturbs her very much. Someone must hold her while the other drives.

Precious has known only gentleness and kindness for a few years now, although my tears have frequently fallen upon her fur, and I do not know what would happen to her if she had to return to a world full of cats like old Tom who never learned an alternative for aggression in order to gain his needs.